What the Moon Said

What the Moon Said

GAYLE ROSENGREN

G. P. Putnam's Sons
An Imprint of Penguin Group (USA)

G. P. PUTNAM'S SONS
Published by the Penguin Group
Penguin Group (USA) LLC
375 Hudson Street, New York, NY 10014

USA | Canada | UK | Ireland | Australia | New Zealand | India | South Africa | China
penguin.com
A Penguin Random House Company

Library of Congress Cataloging-in-Publication Data
Rosengren, Gayle.
What the moon said / Gayle Rosengren.
pages cm
Summary: When Esther's family moves to a farm during the Great Depression,
she soon learns that there are things much more important than that
her superstitious mother rarely shows her any affection.
[1. Farm life—Wisconsin—Fiction. 2. Mothers and daughters—Fiction. 3. Superstition—Fiction.
4. Family life—Wisconsin—Fiction. 5. Depressions—1929—Fiction. 6. Wisconsin—History—
20th century—Fiction.] I. Title.
PZ7.R719268Wh 2014
[Fic]—dc23
2013003442

Printed in the United States of America.
ISBN 978-0-399-16352-4
1 3 5 7 9 10 8 6 4 2

Design by Marikka Tamura.
Text set in Golden Cockerel ITC Std.

In loving memory of my mother and my grandmother—
the real Esther and Ma—
whose lives provided the inspiration for this story.

1 A Ring Around the Moon

ESTHER PLANTED HER FEET ON THE CURB. Her older sister Violet tugged at her arm and said, "Come on! We're going to be late for the matinee."

But Esther wouldn't budge—not until a streetcar had clattered past and the street was empty in both directions.

"Ma said to be extra careful today," she reminded Violet as she finally stepped off the curb and crossed the street. "She saw a ring around the moon last night. That means something bad is going to happen." Almost without thinking, Esther glanced upward. But the only things above the tall buildings were a few puffs of clouds and the sun. No moon with a ring around it. It had been there last night, though. Esther shivered.

1

Violet sniffed. "Ma thinks everything's a sign. Don't take it so seriously."

Esther stopped dead. "Vi! How can you say that? Didn't Ma know Mrs. Straus had her baby before Mr. Straus came to tell us, because she dropped a spoon at supper? And didn't she say someone had died just before we heard about Mr. Bell's accident? She had a dream about a wedding and that always means a death. And—"

"All right!" Violet gave in, raising her hands in surrender. "Ma can read signs. I know that. But if something bad is going to happen, I don't want to know about it ahead of time. Why worry before you have to?"

Esther toed a bit of sawdust that had been tracked from the butcher shop onto the sidewalk. "But," she said slowly, "maybe if you know, you can be so careful that the bad luck passes you by."

"And gets someone else instead," Violet suggested with a laugh, starting to walk again.

Esther followed Violet, frowning. She had never thought of it that way before, but she was proud of Ma for knowing things that other people didn't. She learned growing up in Russia, and it made her special.

If only she were more like Mrs. Rubinstein, Ma would be perfect.

Mrs. Rubinstein was Shirley Rubinstein's mother, and Shirley was Esther's best friend. Shirley sat next to Esther in Miss Monksburg's class. They giggled over lunches, jumped double Dutch at recess, and played jacks and hopscotch after school. Shirley wasn't snooty like a lot of the other girls who lived north of school in nice houses instead of south, in dark apartments. Shirley had dolls and puzzles and books she didn't mind sharing. She even had a miniature china tea set for her dolls. Best of all, though, she had a beautiful mother who hugged Shirley and kissed her cheek every time she went away or came home.

The first time Esther saw this, her heart swelled with envy. Ma did not give kisses. She hardly ever gave hugs. Esther was determined to change that.

When she went home from Shirley's after that first visit, Esther had gone straight to Ma and flung her arms around Ma's waist. Unfortunately, Ma had been washing dishes and hadn't heard Esther coming. The surprise hug startled her. She dropped the pot she was washing and it splashed water all down the front of her dress.

"Esther! What is wrong with you? Look what you did," Ma had scolded.

Esther took a faltering step backward, but she didn't give up. "I just wanted to give you a hug. That's all. Didn't you like it?"

Ma frowned. "Now I must change my dress."

"I'm sorry," Esther said. "Let me give you a kiss to show you how sorry I am." She reached up to grasp Ma's neck and pull her head closer. But Ma pulled away.

"Esther, stop this foolishness! You'll get all wet. If you want to show me how sorry you are, wipe the water off the floor." Then, muttering something in Russian, Ma had gone to her bedroom to change.

Esther still remembered how her cheeks had burned and her eyes had stung as Ma walked away.

Since then, Esther had done a lot of thinking and a lot of watching. She noticed things that had slid past her before—like how Ma did hug the older girls, Kate and Julia. She even hugged her little brother, Walter, and Violet sometimes. Not often, but sometimes. With a jolt that had shaken her heart, Esther realized that she couldn't remember the last time Ma had hugged *her*. Didn't Ma love her as much as she loved Walter and Violet?

Esther tried to think why this would be. Was it because Violet and Walter and the older girls looked like Pa, with his lighter hair and gray eyes? Esther couldn't help it if she had dark hair and eyes and looked more like Ma's family. Once, Aunt Olga even said that Esther could have been the twin of their little sister Tatiana. Ma's face had gone white and she'd snapped something in Russian that made Aunt Olga bite her lip and apologize. Why? Esther had wondered. Hadn't Ma liked Tatiana? But Esther couldn't imagine Ma not liking—*loving*—her own sister. There had to be a different reason why Ma had gotten so upset and why she didn't want to hug Esther.

In the end, Esther decided that the reason didn't

matter. The important thing was to change Ma's mind—to *make* her want to hug Esther. But changing Ma's mind was never easy.

Esther knew she would need all the help she could get. So she made lots and lots of wishes. She wished on first stars. She wished on chicken wishbones whenever she won the larger half away from Walter or Violet. She wished on a penny she found glinting in the school yard one sunny day. She even wished on a four-leaf clover she discovered poking up through a crack in the sidewalk in front of the library. Best of all, soon she would wish with all her might on her birthday candles. She would wish for Ma to hug her just like Mrs. Rubinstein hugged Shirley. Then Esther would know for sure that Ma loved her as much as her brother and sisters.

"Hurry up, Es!" Violet said. "Why are you so slow today? We're going to be late."

"Sorry," Esther said, and she quickened her pace.

The girls turned the corner onto Clark Street. A long, straggly line of people was blocking much of the sidewalk. At the head of the line, two ladies were serving up bowls of soup and slices of bread. Most of the people shuffling forward for food were grime-coated men. They had hunched shoulders and shaggy heads. But a few were women. Their heads were bowed as if their scarves were too heavy. And there were children in the soup line, too, squirming and whimpering, impatient to get to the food. One of them reminded Esther of Walter. The boy had the same wiry hair and stick-out ears. But his face was pale and thin, not rosy and chubby-cheeked like her little brother's.

"I wish they'd never opened this ol' soup kitchen," Violet muttered, taking Esther's arm to steer her firmly around the line. "All the beggars in the city come here now."

Esther wanted to say it was good that the hungry people were getting food, but she kept silent. Violet was only repeating what Ma had said so many times. Ma thought it was shameful for people to take charity instead of earning their own food.

Esther was glad when they left the soup line behind. Seeing it always made her feel guilty. Her family had plenty to eat. Most Saturdays she and Violet even got to see a movie. Now the Diversey Theater was just ahead and the matinee was about to begin.

Esther and Violet hurried past the bakery, past the shoemaker's shop, and past the secondhand store. They paid their nickels to the man at the door of the theater and scooted inside.

When the screen flickered to life a few minutes later, Esther laughed along with everyone else at the Marx Brothers' silliness. But later, when the film ended and some people in the audience left the theater, she sat up straighter. Her favorite part of the matinee was about to begin—the adventure serial, starring Rin Tin Tin the Wonder Dog.

Rin Tin Tin—Rinty for short—was a hero. He risked his life to save people. Today's episode, "Jaws of Peril," began with him rescuing his mistress Delores from a burning building. She'd been trapped there in the last episode by crooks who wanted to steal her father's gold mine. Rinty saved her, and then he saved Buzz, the neighbor boy, from a well where he surely would have drowned.

All the while, the bad guys were after Rinty, because he was the only one who could lead them to the gold mine. They came up with a cruel plan to get rid of Marco, the mysterious stranger who had fallen in love with Delores. They captured Rinty and tied him up. Then they left a wild dog in his place. When Marco returned, the wild dog attacked him!

The audience gasped.

Across the hall, Rinty heard Marco's cries for help. Esther watched breathlessly as he clawed and scratched and finally wrenched himself free of the ropes that were holding him. Then he raced to where Marco was fighting for his life.

Rin Tin Tin leaped on the wild dog. The two of them rolled and wrestled and snarled.

Esther jumped up. "Get him, Rinty! Get him!" she screamed.

A hard yank on her skirt tumbled her back into her seat just as the screen went still.

The announcer's voice boomed, "Don't miss the next episode of *The Lone Defender* with Rin Tin Tin the Wonder Dog!" Music blared. The lights came on.

Esther blinked against the sudden brightness. "I can't wait!" she wailed. "I have to know if Rin Tin Tin will be all right."

Violet snorted. "Of course he'll be all right. He's always all right. He got himself and Delores out of the burning building from last time, didn't he?"

Esther shrugged, not wanting to agree with her older sister. Twelve-year-old Violet didn't love Rin Tin Tin the way Esther did. She only stayed to watch him because of Esther. And now she was buttoning her coat. Time to go.

"Let's stop by the laundry," Violet suggested, joining the crowd leaving the theater. "Maybe Pa will give us money for ice cream."

Esther's mouth watered even as she shook her head. "Ma only gave him enough for the streetcar. And she told him he should walk and save the nickel if he could."

Violet sighed. "Ma's getting worse and worse," she grumbled. "If it weren't for Julia, we wouldn't even have money for the movies."

Esther nodded, smiling as she thought of good-natured Julia. She was always doing nice things for her younger sisters. She was never too tired, not even after she'd worked a long shift at the telephone company. She curled Esther's flyaway brown hair. She helped Violet with her arithmetic. And she gave them the nickels and dimes Ma would not. Ma held tight to every spare penny. "Making a nest egg," she called it.

"Let's go see Pa anyway," Esther said. "He likes it when we surprise him."

Violet bobbed her head in agreement.

"And maybe Old Nick will be there," Esther added. She saw Violet roll her eyes, but she didn't care. Mr. Zeigler's black terrier was such a friendly little dog. While she was petting him, Esther pretended he was hers. When Esther grew up, she was going to have a dog just like Rin Tin Tin. She'd have a cat, too, and maybe even a horse. But until then, she had to be content with petting other people's animals. Ma had grown up on a farm. She said animals belonged outside. That meant no pets for Esther.

Esther had to take little skips every few steps to keep up with Violet. She was small, like Ma, and she hated it. She'd be ten in a few weeks, but people always thought she was younger. Pa said her eyes were the only big thing about her. Now those eyes caught sight of a car turning the corner just ahead. Esther squinted to see it better.

"Look!" she cried. "That's the Rubinsteins' car. So Shirley *is* still in Chicago. That Leo Bartello and his stories! Just because she was absent the last few days, he said

Shirley had moved away." Esther made a face. "I told him she wouldn't move without telling me."

Violet stopped. She was frowning. "I'm sorry, Es," she said. "I thought you knew. That may have been the Rubinsteins' Studebaker, but that wasn't them. Something went wrong with Mr. Rubinstein's business. They sold their car and their house and moved away, just like Leo said."

Esther couldn't believe it. Many families she knew had moved away in recent months. Their fathers had lost their jobs and they hadn't been able to pay their rent. They'd had to move in with relatives or friends. But these had been poor families. The Rubinsteins were rich!

Esther glared at Violet. "You're wrong!"

But Violet shook her head. "No, it's true. Remember Ma sent me to buy stew meat this morning?"

Esther nodded impatiently. "So?"

"While I was waiting in line at the butcher shop, I heard Mrs. McGuire and Mrs. Pulaski talking about it."

Esther's lip quivered. Mr. McGuire was a policeman, so Mrs. McGuire always knew everything that was going on in the neighborhood. "They really moved away?"

Violet squeezed Esther's shoulder. "I'm sorry," she said again.

"I never even got to say good-bye," Esther said around the lump in her throat.

At Zeigler's Laundry, Esther's sadness over Shirley was

forgotten for a while when Old Nick ran up to her, wagging his stubby tail. He remembered her! She crouched down to pet him. "Nice dog," she crooned. "Good Old Nick."

"I don't see Pa," Violet said, rising up on her toes to see better.

Esther stood up to look, too. She peered around the huge, steaming gray tubs. Pools of water were everywhere and the wet concrete was slippery. Esther eyed it wistfully. Pa had told her more than once not to slide on it. But Pa was not there. Esther ran a few steps and slid. It was so much fun, she did it again. "Wheeee!" she squealed. "Come on, Vi. Slide with me!"

At that moment, the door to the office opened. Esther froze. Pa and Mr. Zeigler came out. Mr. Zeigler had one hand on Pa's back.

"I'm sorry, Chris," Mr. Zeigler said. "You're a good worker. I don't want to let you go. But my wife's brother arrives in two weeks and he'll need a job. What can I do?"

Esther gasped. Violet's mouth fell open. The girls stared at each other. Pa was losing his job! Without a word, they scurried away before Pa could see them.

Outside, they slumped down onto the curb. A gray horse plodded past, pulling a wagon full of ice blocks packed in sawdust. Gray horses were Esther's favorite, but she barely glanced at this one. "Pa can get another job, can't he?" she asked Violet.

Violet waited until the wagon had rumbled past. "Sure, I guess," she said. "But lately jobs are harder to find. That's why there are so many people in the soup line. They can't find work. You've heard the news on the radio every night. You know all the trouble there's been with banks and businesses closing. That's what happened to Shirley's father."

Esther had indeed heard the news each night. Pa would not think of missing it. He and Ma often talked about it afterward, too—about the hard times that were coming. And Esther had felt truly sorry for the people who would suffer. But she'd never imagined hard times would come to them. She felt foolish now, but somehow she'd thought they were safe from the trouble that threatened everyone else. She had always *felt* safe. Until now.

2 A Decision

"WHAT WILL HAPPEN IF PA CAN'T FIND another job?" Esther's voice quivered, and she knew tears were not far away. Would her family be put out of their apartment like the Kozlowskis had been? Would all their furniture, even their beds, be piled on the sidewalk? Would they soon be joining those people in the soup line? Would they be hungry and dirty, with no home and no food? Esther remembered the boy with the thin, pale cheeks. Her heart beat so hard, she could barely breathe. Could such a horrible thing happen to her family?

"Ma and Pa will think of something," Violet told her. But Esther heard the worry in her sister's voice. It made her more frightened than ever.

Slowly, they climbed the stairs to their third-floor apartment. The little bells above the front door tinkled when they opened it, and Ma looked up from her dusting. She could tell from their faces that something bad had happened. She dropped her dust cloth and asked, "What is it? What's wrong?"

Violet told Ma what they'd overheard. Esther stood trembling beside Violet. If only Ma would hug her and say, "It will be all right." That would make the trembling stop, Esther was sure. And if Ma loved Esther more, she might say and do these things. But Ma did not love her enough. Not yet.

"I vas afraid something like this vould happen," Ma moaned, sinking onto the nearest chair. When Ma was upset, she slipped back to pronouncing *w*'s like *v*'s, as they were in the Old Country. "That ring," she continued, wringing her hands. "I knew it vould bring us trouble."

Suddenly Esther remembered. The ring around the moon Ma had seen the night before! "You knew." She looked at Ma with wide eyes. "You *always* know. Will you teach me how to read signs, too? Please, Ma."

But Ma was staring out the window. She didn't seem to hear. Esther finally gave up and went to tell her doll, Margaret, the terrible news.

Pa and Julia arrived together that night, and Esther could tell by the pinched edges of Julia's smile that she'd already heard the news. Julia sat beside Esther at the table and gave her hand a quick squeeze. Pa walked across the room with slumped shoulders. When Walter ran up for Pa to swing him in the air, Pa just patted his head.

"Zeigler has to let me go," he told Ma, each word sounding heavy and tired. "Two more weeks and I will be without work."

Pa wasn't afraid of anything, not even the biggest, ugliest spiders. But Esther heard fear in his voice now, and her heart shuddered.

Ma set a pot of stew on the table. "Sit. Eat," she said in a softer than usual voice. "It will be all right." Here were the words that Esther had longed to hear earlier, but Pa's face still looked worried, so they did not bring as much comfort as she'd expected.

There was never much conversation at the Vogel table. Ma believed children shouldn't speak during meals unless they were spoken to. That was how it had been when she grew up in Russia. Pa sometimes told a story about something that had happened at the laundry. Ma sometimes shared bits of neighborhood news. But meals were mostly quiet.

That night the quiet was different. It was so thick, it seemed to press around Esther like a blanket. Only it wasn't warm and comforting like the blanket on her bed. It was heavy and hot and made her desperate to shove it away. Only the clink of silverware and the creak of chairs disturbed it. Esther found herself purposely making more noise with her fork than she needed to. Ma glanced sharply at her once, but she did not scold. Perhaps the silence bothered her, too.

Esther wasn't hungry. She had to force herself to chew and swallow, chew and swallow. Ma expected everyone to eat everything on their plates, always. Food was not to be wasted. Finally, Ma and Pa stood up and went into the parlor. When no one was looking, Esther spat her last mouthful of food into the garbage pail. Then she helped Violet with the dishes while Julia put Walter to bed. But her gaze kept returning to the closed parlor door.

"They're still in there," Esther said when the last spoon was dried and put away.

"I wonder what they're saying," Violet said, edging a little nearer to the door.

"We'll find out soon enough," Julia observed, coming back into the kitchen. "No snooping, Violet Vogel."

Violet flushed and backed away from the door. But she complained, "It's not fair that they're talking in the parlor. We can't listen to the radio. And it's time for *The Smith Family*!" *The Smith Family* was the Vogel family's favorite show. Pa never missed it.

"It can't be helped," Julia said. "But we can still have fun. Why don't we play rummy?"

"The cards are in the parlor," Violet reminded her.

Julia bit her lip. "That's right. I wasn't thinking. Well then, why don't we read at the table? That will be fun, too."

Esther was quick to agree, but Violet made a face.

"Oh, come on," Esther told her. "Julia's right. It'll be fun."

"For you, maybe," Violet said, but she trudged after Esther to their bedroom.

Violet brought her writing tablet and a pencil back to the kitchen. She sighed. "I have a composition to write for Monday. I might as well start it now."

Esther opened her library book, but the story wasn't as exciting as she remembered. It couldn't keep her attention from wandering back to the parlor. What was being said there? Would Ma and Pa think of a place where Pa might find work?

The minute hand crawled around the kitchen clock. Half an hour passed. Forty-five minutes. Esther quit trying to read. She set her book down. Violet had stopped writing to gaze at the parlor door. Julia was doing the same thing.

Finally, the door opened and Ma and Pa appeared. The slump in Pa's shoulders was gone.

"Ma and I have made a decision," he announced. "We are going to buy a farm." His gray eyes sparkled with excitement. "We have been saving for a long time to buy a house here in Chicago. But with times so bad, cities are not a good place to be. Better to move to the country. Better to have our own land and work for ourselves."

Ma nodded in agreement, although her dark eyes were sober. "It will not be easy," she said, "but it can be a good life for us. A better life."

Esther stared at them, too astonished to speak. Live on a farm? In the *country*?

"But Ma," Julia protested, "we can't just leave Chicago. All our family and friends are here. And my job. Besides, we aren't farmers."

"I was a farmer until I left Germany," Pa reminded her. "I can be a farmer again."

Esther tried to picture it. "Will the farm be far away?" she asked.

"I have to find it first, *Liebling*," Pa said. "But I hope not too far."

Violet looked sick. "Will we go soon? What if we don't like it? Can we come back?"

Ma frowned. "You ask too many questions," she said. "It is late. There will be plenty of time to talk tomorrow. Now it is time for bed."

When they all just stared at her, she made a shooing motion with her hands. *"Nu?"* This was a Russian word that meant "Well?" The way Ma had said it meant she was annoyed. "What did I say? Good night!"

The girls knew better than to argue. But when Esther

and Violet slipped into the bed they shared a few minutes later, Violet choked out, "A farm! How can Pa be so h-happy? It will be awful!"

Esther tried to comfort her. "Pa and Ma must know what's best," she said. She didn't dare say what she was really thinking—that on a farm there were bound to be animals. Cows. Horses. Maybe even a dog. Of course, it would mean leaving her school, her teacher . . . and all her friends. An unexpected sob swelled in her throat. Tears filled her eyes.

Even with animals, would Esther really like living on a farm? She had always lived in Chicago. She didn't know what it was like to live anyplace else. Would there be towns near the farm with schools and ice cream shops? Would there be a library? And what about movie theaters? Why, she might never find out what happened to Rin Tin Tin in the final episode of *The Lone Defender*! Esther felt hot tears rolling down her cheeks. Violet was right. It was going to be awful. And all because of some horrid old ring around the moon!

3 Moving Day

FROM THE STREET BELOW, A PEDDLER called, "Po-*taaay*-toes! Fine po-*taaay*-toes!" His horse's hooves clip-clopped on the pavement.

Esther sat up in bed and scrabbled beneath the sheet until she found Margaret. The doll had been a gift from Kate and Julia the Christmas Esther was five. Margaret had golden curls, a frilly pink dress, even real satin slippers. Esther had never seen a doll so beautiful. As the years passed, first one and then the other of her tiny shoes had been lost. Her dress had grown faded and worn. And her curls had gone limp from brushing. But Esther still thought Margaret was beautiful. She especially loved the doll's china-blue eyes. They never failed to look interested in whatever Esther had to say.

"Today's the day we move to the farm," she whispered, hugging Margaret close. "But don't be scared. Julia says it's going to be a great adventure. I just wish she was coming with us." Esther sighed. Julia had convinced Ma and Pa to let her stay behind with Kate. Kate was the oldest sister in the Vogel family. She was ten whole years older than Esther, and she was married. She and her husband, Howard, had an apartment with an extra bedroom.

"I can be company for Kate when Howard works at night," Julia had pleaded. "And I can keep my job at the telephone company." Both reasons were true enough. But Esther knew there was another reason Julia wanted to stay in Chicago. She didn't want to leave David. David was a tall young man with laughing eyes and crinkly red hair. He and Julia planned to be married as soon as they saved up enough money.

Esther hugged Margaret tighter. She didn't want to say good-bye to Julia. Julia was the sister she was closest to, even if Violet was nearer to her in age. She and Violet were very different. Violet didn't love books. She didn't enjoy school. She didn't like animals. And she didn't pretend things in her head the way Esther did.

"What's the point?" Violet would say. And Esther didn't know how to explain the magic of pretending. Julia understood without explaining. She spun daydreams right along with Esther—dreams of riding an elephant, or singing on the radio, even flying an airplane like Amelia Earhart!

"Now you're going to have a real adventure," Julia told Esther the night before the move. "And you must write to me and tell me all about it."

Esther's spirits had lifted at that. She'd never had anyone to write letters to before. "Will you write back?" she asked.

Julia laughed. "Of course I will! Just wait and see."

Remembering Julia's promise, Esther cheered up. It would be fun to get letters. And it would be fun to have a real adventure instead of just pretend ones.

"Es!" Violet hissed, poking her head into the room. "Ma's looking for you."

Esther dropped Margaret and scrambled out of bed. Ma thought Esther was too old for dolls. She said so more and more often lately. She wouldn't be happy if she found Esther playing with Margaret on such a busy morning. Esther snatched clean underwear from her drawer and hurried into the bathroom. A few minutes later, dressed in yesterday's jumper with a fresh white blouse, Esther started for the kitchen, where Ma and Pa were talking.

"In the dream it was as if Tatiana was trying to warn me," she heard Ma say fretfully.

Tatiana! Esther stopped abruptly. That was the sister

Aunt Olga said Esther looked like. What had Ma dreamed about her?

"Did she speak to you?" Pa asked. "What did she say?"

"She did not speak. She just stood there with a suitcase in her hand."

"That doesn't sound so terrible," Pa replied.

"But it had been raining. Rain at the start of a journey is always an omen of bad fortune. Maybe—maybe the move is a mistake." Esther had never heard Ma sound so uncertain.

"Sometimes a dream is just a dream, Anna," said Pa. "Besides, you say it *had* been raining. So the rain had stopped. The sun was probably about to come out. That would make it a dream of *good* fortune."

"Maybe you are right . . . ," Ma said.

"Of course I am," Pa said. "Now, no more worries. I must go watch for the movers."

Esther listened to his footsteps go out of the apartment and down the stairs before she went into the kitchen. Ma was wrapping plates in old newspaper and stacking them in a metal washtub. Esther was relieved to hear her humming softly under her breath. She must have decided that Pa was right and this time a dream was just a dream.

"There you are!" Ma said when she saw Esther. "You must hurry and eat. The movers will be here soon and there is still much work to be done."

Esther ate the slice of homemade bread Ma had set out for her. She drank her glass of milk. And all the while she watched Ma. How quickly her hands flew from one plate to the next. Already the tub was nearly full. The next time Esther saw those plates, she'd be in the new house on the farm. She'd have begun her first real adventure.

Impulsively, Esther said, "It's an exciting day, isn't it, Ma?"

Ma's hands paused at their work. She looked surprised by Esther's question. But she nodded. "Yes. A very exciting day." Her voice was soft. A smile played at the corners of her mouth. Esther smiled back at her. It was as if she and Ma shared a special secret.

"Can I help you pack the dishes, Ma?" she asked. If Ma said yes, she'd work her hardest and fastest. Then Ma might say, "*Nu*, Esther, what would I do without you?" She might even give Esther a hug. Barely breathing, Esther waited for Ma's reply.

But Ma shook her head. "No. You go help Violet with the bedding."

Esther was disappointed. But obedience was as important to Ma as hard work. So Esther said, "Yes, Ma," and hurried to the bedroom. She helped Violet tie the corners of their sheets together with pillows, quilt, and blankets—even Margaret!—all snug inside. It made a big, bulging bundle too awkward for them to carry, but not for Pa. He picked it up as if it were a bag of rolls and went away whistling.

Esther guessed from the sound of his whistling that he had liked being a farmer. And anything that Pa liked so well, she would like, too, she decided. Suddenly she couldn't wait to see the farm in Wisconsin. Only Pa had been there, but he came back with glowing eyes.

"Good land," he'd said to Ma. "It is good land."

"And the house?" she asked.

He blinked and shrugged. "Fine. The house is fine."

A little crease had appeared between Ma's eyebrows. "There are enough rooms? There is a stove?"

Pa had waved his hand and nodded. "Yes, yes, Anna. We will have everything we need. Do not worry. Life will be good."

Until that morning, Esther had mostly thought of the bad things about moving. But both Ma and Pa were so happy and hopeful. Life on the farm really might be better than life in the city. And if life was better, Ma would be happier. Why, she was already happier, and they hadn't even moved yet. Once they were actually living on the farm, she would probably smile all the time. It would be easy for Esther to slip her arm around Ma's waist and hug her. Then, surely, Ma would hug her back. Esther's heart beat faster just thinking about it.

When the three big moving men arrived, they carried beds, dressers, tables, and chairs outside. They loaded them onto their truck. Pa and Howard helped. They carried lamps, mirrors, and dishes Ma wouldn't trust to the movers. Esther was not surprised to see Pa carry the radio downstairs himself, too. She looked out the window and saw him gently set it in the back of the truck. He pointed to it and said something to one of the movers. She guessed that he was telling him to take very good care of it.

Pa had saved up months of streetcar fares to buy the radio from Mr. Greenberg's secondhand store. He'd traded his Victrola and records, too. When he brought the radio home, Esther, Violet, and Julia had been delighted. Ma had raised her eyebrows, but the radio had stayed.

Every night after supper, Pa listened to the news. Then they all listened to the funny radio shows and laughed together. Later still, when Esther and Violet were going to bed, Pa listened to music. Pa loved all kinds of music, but he especially loved waltzes.

Ma called the radio a waste of money. But she listened to it, too. She smiled at the silly programs and she scowled at the news—especially if it mentioned President Hoover. Ma blamed the president for all the bad things happening in the country.

Best of all, though, Ma enjoyed the music. Esther didn't realize just how much until one night when she got out of bed to get a drink of water and saw Ma and Pa waltzing around the parlor. She'd never seen Ma look so happy.

Moving was hard work, Esther discovered. She and Violet scurried around, sweeping each room as it was emptied. Kate made sandwiches for their lunch and supper. Julia scrubbed the bathroom. Ma cleaned the icebox and the stove. Even Walter was put to work dusting baseboards and windowsills. The apartment had to be left clean for the new tenants.

Finally the last box was loaded onto the truck. The last room was swept. The last sandwich was put in the basket. The bathroom and kitchen were spotless. Only then did Ma take the cross from its place of honor on the shelf in the parlor. Carefully, she wrapped it in a soft cloth and tucked it into her purse.

Ma's father had given the cross to her when she had left Russia to sail across the ocean to America. "To keep you safe," he had told her as he pressed it into her hands. Ma had told Esther and Violet the story many times. How she had been sad to leave her father and little brothers and sisters even though she was excited to come to America. The iron cross had comforted her on the long journey and during hard times in all the years since.

"My father had the village blacksmith make the cross out of iron so it would have the strongest powers of protection," she explained. "And he had my poor dead mother's red enamel cross set in its center to always remind me of her."

The tiny red cross in the center of the bigger one made Esther think of a heart. She knew the iron cross had very strong powers, but she liked to think that her grandmother's little one gave it extra-special power to protect their family and home.

Last of all, on their way out of the apartment, Pa reached up and plucked free the string of tiny bells that hung above the door and tinkled every time the door opened or closed. They jingled as he dropped them into his jacket pocket.

Pa would soon be hanging the bells above the door of the farmhouse. Fairies loved the sound of bells, and having them ringing on the threshold of the house—right where the fairies lived—would make them happy.

Happy fairies were a good thing. Unhappy fairies were not, and they could cause bad things to happen to the humans who were their neighbors. Sometimes little things like skinned knees and lost gloves. But bigger things, too, like fires and sickness. Ma would never spend a night in a house without bells above the door and her cross standing guard within.

"Time to go," Pa said. He touched Julia's cheek. "We will miss you."

Julia sniffled.

Always impatient with tears, Ma said, "*Nu*—I thought you wanted to stay!"

Julia half laughed, half sobbed. "I did. I do. But I'll miss you all terribly." She hugged Violet. Then she hugged Esther. "Don't forget to write," she said into Esther's ear.

Esther felt something being pressed into her hand. A coin.

Julia curled Esther's fingers over it. "For postage," she whispered. Esther hugged Julia hard, her throat too tight to speak.

Howard had borrowed his brother's old Buick to drive them to the farm. Pa sat up front with him, and Walter sat between them. The backseat was more crowded because at the last minute Kate decided to ride along.

"I want to see the farm," she said. "And this way I can be company for Howard on the ride home." So Ma, Kate, Violet, and Esther all squeezed in together.

Usually Esther thought any automobile ride was a treat. But this one was too crowded right from the start. On top of that, Kate and Ma talked on and on about babies. Kate was going to have her first baby at the end of summer. She had lots of questions. Ma knew all the answers. She knew what to feed babies, how to dress them, what to do when they cried. Kate seemed fascinated. But Esther and Violet rolled their eyes at each other.

Esther looked out the window. She watched the city buildings slip away behind them. She saw more and more open fields and trees ahead. But they had a very long way to go. Over one hundred miles!

They stopped once at a roadside picnic area. They ate some of the sandwiches Kate had made and washed them down with cold water. Then Ma made Esther and Violet and Walter use the outhouse. It wasn't a real bathroom, just a tiny wooden shack. And it didn't have a real toilet that flushed. It just had a hole cut into a wooden bench.

Esther hated it because it smelled and there were spiderwebs in all the corners.

She held her breath and hurried as fast as she could. Esther feared all bugs, but spiders most of all. She was glad when her family climbed back into the car. It might be crowded, but at least it didn't smell, and there were no spiders to worry about.

After a while, Violet's eyelids drooped. Esther closed her eyes, too, but not to sleep. She wanted to daydream about life on the farm. Her mind was like the screen at the movie theater, except it showed pictures in color, not just black and white. She saw rolling green fields, an apple orchard, a splashing brook. She saw a big red barn, a fat brown cow, two prancing gray horses, and dozens of chickens. She saw a snug white house with green shutters. And best of all, she saw a dog dozing on the porch steps. The dog looked just like Rin Tin Tin . . .

"Here!" came Pa's voice. "Here is where we turn. Our farm is just ahead."

Esther awakened with a start. She had fallen asleep after all! She sat up straight and blinked quickly as they bumped down a rutted dirt road. Everyone was leaning forward in their seats, straining to catch a glimpse of their new home. Esther leaned forward, too, to peer around Ma and look out the side window. But when she saw her mother's face, she stared at Ma instead.

Ma's cheeks were flushed. Her eyes were bright. Her nose was so close to the glass, her breath made a foggy cloud on it. And the corners of her mouth were curved up expectantly. She looked as happy as when she'd been waltzing with Pa. Esther had been right. Ma was going to be different here. Everything was going to be different here!

But as Esther watched, Ma's mouth sagged. Her eyes closed. She drew back sharply from the window. A chill skipped up the back of Esther's neck. What was wrong? She looked out where Ma had been looking. She saw bare black fields, an old faded-pink barn, and some crumbling sheds. Off to the right was another building. It was small and shabby, the color of ashes. Esther's chest tightened. She squinted and craned her neck, but there was nothing else to see. That shabby gray building had to be their house.

Disappointment swelled from her chest to her throat and stuck there. All of Ma's hard-saved nest egg had gone for this? She had to be even more disappointed than Esther. Impulsively, Esther reached out to give Ma's arm a loving squeeze. But just at that moment, Ma stiffened. She raised her chin and she set her mouth in such a grim line that Esther jerked her hand back.

The car stopped near the barn and Pa jumped out. He pointed to the fields. "Only thirty acres," he said, "but enough for a start." He led them into the barn. He pointed out the wagon and buggy, the plow, and other tools. "All this is ours," he said proudly.

Best of all were the animals. The two big workhorses were brown, not gray. And the four cows were black with white spots, not brown as Esther had imagined. But she didn't care. They were *real*. They let Esther pat them. One cow bobbed her head as if to say, "Howdy-do." Both horses nickered gently. Esther's disappointment in the house was forgotten. Horses! They owned horses! She couldn't wait to ride them.

"We have to name them," she said excitedly.

"Later," Ma said. Then she turned and stalked out the door. After a stunned moment, everyone trotted after her.

Ma marched right past the sheds. Pa pointed out the pigsty. He pointed out the henhouse. And he pointed out the icehouse where he would cool and separate the milk. But he didn't stop again, because Ma was moving ever faster toward the house. He must have realized some-thing was wrong. He walked faster, too. His long legs caught up with her just as she reached the front door. Pa took a key from his pocket, put it in the lock, and opened the door. Then they went quickly inside.

Esther and Violet weren't far behind and would have followed Ma and Pa into the house, but Kate called to them to wait. When she and Howard joined the girls on the porch a few moments later, Kate said, "Let's give Ma and Pa a little time alone." Holding on to Howard's arm, she walked gingerly across the sagging porch, shaking her head. "Oh, Pa," she sighed.

Esther bit her lip. Things weren't going at all the way she had imagined. Of course, the house might be much nicer inside than it was outside. It might. She crossed her fingers and tried to peek through a window. But it was so coated with dirt, she couldn't see a thing. Meanwhile, Walter was running dizzily around the house, blowing a whistle he'd pulled from his pocket. Violet was staring at the empty fields with a bleak expression. And Howard was trying to cheer up Kate.

"It's not so bad," he said heartily. "A little paint and a good cleaning and it'll be real cozy." But Esther could tell he didn't mean it. He was smiling too hard. And Kate's raised eyebrows said she didn't believe Howard, either.

Ma and Pa finally came out. Ma's back was very straight. Her mouth was very tight. It was Pa who invited everyone in to see the new house. "After the first harvest I will fix it up," he told them. "Until then, it will do."

Esther and Violet went through the house together. It didn't take long. There were only three rooms downstairs—the kitchen, the parlor, and a bedroom for Ma and Pa. Upstairs there were two small rooms with sloping ceilings—one for the girls and one for Walter.

"Where's the bathroom, Pa?" Violet called down.

"Out back," he said. He added quickly over Violet's shrieks, "Just until the first harvest. It will not be so bad. Be thankful it is spring."

Esther shivered at the thought of using an outhouse in winter. Then she imagined using it in summer and shivered even harder. There would be all kinds of horrible bugs!

The toot of a horn announced the arrival of the truck with their furniture. Esther trudged down the stairs after Violet. Ma and Pa went out to greet the movers. But Esther stopped to look more closely at the kitchen. It didn't look like any kitchen she'd ever seen.

"Where's the icebox?" she whispered to Kate. Surely it wasn't outside, too!

Kate sighed. "There doesn't seem to be one."

Esther felt her mouth fall open. No icebox! "How will we keep our food cold?"

"There's a cellar." Kate pointed to a small door in the middle of the floor.

Esther's "oh" was very soft. Things were getting worse and worse.

"And I may as well tell you, while Ma and Pa are out-side—there's no electricity, either." Kate rubbed between her eyes as if she had a headache.

"That does it! We can't stay here," Violet objected. "Nobody lives like this anymore!" She stomped her foot indignantly.

"Shush! Ma and Pa will hear," Kate said with a worried glance at the door. "Look, I know it's bad. It's not what anyone expected, least of all Ma. But it was the only farm Pa could afford and he's so excited about it . . ." She smiled encouragingly. "Give it a chance. Maybe it won't be so bad."

"Easy for you to say," Violet said sourly. "You don't have to go outside to the bathroom. And you'll still have—"

"The radio!" Esther suddenly gasped. "Without electricity we can't listen to the radio."

Kate groaned. Violet actually whimpered. Esther felt the last bits of hope drain out of her, like air from a dying balloon. This was not an adventure; it was a disaster. And there was no going back. Like it or not, this was their new home. Esther looked at the peeling walls, the water-stained ceilings, and the cracked linoleum floor. Ma would never become more like Mrs. Rubinstein in this horrible place! Never.

A sob was crawling its way up her throat, but Esther wouldn't let it out. They were here to stay. There had to be a way to make it good. Esther rubbed furiously at a grimy window with the cuff of her coat. She cleaned a big circle and looked out. In the distance she saw the bare black fields. They'd be green before long. And Howard was right about the house. Some scrubbing and paint would brighten it a lot. It might not be so awful then. In time, they might even get to like it.

Esther closed her eyes tight. She imagined the house bright and snug and clean. Good smells wafting out of the kitchen. Pa working out in the fields. Ma waving to him from the porch. And Esther standing beside Ma, with her arm around Ma's waist and Ma's arm around her shoulders . . .

Esther opened her eyes and blinked. For a moment she'd thought Ma had come up behind her. Then she realized it was her own reflection she was seeing in the glass. It was her uplifted chin. It was her squared shoulders. Things hadn't turned out the way she'd expected. But that didn't mean Esther was going to give up. It might take a little longer here to make Ma love Esther enough to hug her like Mrs. Rubinstein hugged Shirley. But Esther would work and wish harder than ever to make it happen.

4 A Friend

AFTER AN EARLY SUPPER OF COLD
sandwiches, Howard and Kate left for home. It would be
late when they reached Chicago again. Esther stood on
the porch with the rest of the family and waved good-
bye. As the car drove away, she tried not to feel frightened. They were really on their own now. There was no
way to go back. Then Pa hammered the string of fairy
bells above the door, and Esther felt better.

"Church tomorrow," Ma said. "Everyone inside for
baths."

Esther looked at her in surprise. "But we don't have a
bathroom—or a bathtub."

"Yes, we do." Ma disappeared into the small enclosed
porch that connected to the kitchen. It was like a pantry

and storage closet combined. When Ma came back, she had the gray metal tub she'd stacked dishes in that morning.

Walter giggled. "That's for laundry."

"And for baths," Ma said firmly. Then she asked Pa to pound some nails into the walls. In a few minutes she had a clothesline strung across the middle of the kitchen. She hung a sheet over the line so it made a kind of wall. "Nu," she said to Esther. "Here is your bathroom. Now, who will be first?"

Walter was first. Esther was second. Fascinated, she watched Ma fill the tub with warm water from the big tank on the side of the stove. Ma called it a reservoir, and she dipped into it with the biggest dipper Esther had ever seen. When the tub was ready, Esther stepped in and sat down. She couldn't quite straighten her legs. The tub was too short. But it was big enough to wash in. Ma handed Esther the bar of Ivory soap she kept just for Saturday night baths. Then she opened the oven door so hot air puffed out around Esther, and she felt all warm and cozy.

"Hurry," Ma reminded her from the sink, where she was washing dishes.

Esther ran the soapy washrag up and down her arms and legs. But all the while she was looking around the kitchen. It was very different from their kitchen in Chicago. The stove was much bigger and burned wood instead of coal, so there was a basket full of sticks in the corner. And the sink didn't have hot and cold water faucets. It had a pump. Ma had to work the pump handle up and down before water splashed out. Then she had to watch the bucket under the sink so it didn't overflow, because there was no drainpipe to carry the water away. When the bucket was full, it had to be emptied outside.

"We're like pioneers," Esther said suddenly, "aren't we, Ma?" It was a surprising thought, but also an exciting one. Pioneers had real adventures all the time. Their life was hard, but they were brave and hardworking. They were—what was the word her teacher used sometimes? *Self-reliant*, that was it. Pioneers were self-reliant. They didn't need other people. They didn't need electricity or even bathrooms. They built homes and farms where before there had been nothing at all.

Pioneers could do anything, Esther guessed. Pioneers could easily make this farm prosper, and make the farmhouse a cozy and cheerful place. And a pioneer girl, even one who was small for her age, could work very hard. She could be so hardworking and helpful, her mother couldn't help but love her as much as her brother and sisters.

Ma muttered something about pioneers that Esther couldn't quite hear. Then she raised her voice and said, "Are you finished yet? Violet is waiting." Esther sighed and reached for the towel. It was clear Ma was still a long way from being happy. When she spoke to Pa, her voice was stiff and chilly. Esther tried not to think about it.

Instead, she pretended she was a pioneer girl. As she dried herself off and tugged her nightgown over her head, she pretended she heard wolves howling in the distance. Or maybe it was Indians . . . !

That night, Esther went to bed by the light of a kerosene lamp in her new room in her new house. She felt odd, almost as if she really had turned into a pioneer girl. She was glad to climb into her same old bed with Violet just like always. And she was very glad to have Margaret to hug to her cheek when she closed her eyes.

The next morning, as she sat down to breakfast, Violet grumbled, "My shoes are too small. I'll get blisters walking all the way to town."

"Pa said it's not far," Esther said quickly. Violet glared at her, but Esther didn't care. She was eager to see town, especially the school. She didn't want Violet's possible blisters to delay the trip.

"We will not walk," Ma said. "We will take the buggy."

Esther was so excited by this unexpected announcement that she dropped her bread, jam-side down, on the floor. Ma shook her head at such clumsiness, and Esther's cheeks burned. But she'd never ridden in a buggy before! She threw the bread in the pail of food scraps that would go to the pigs. Then she wiped up the floor with a damp rag from under the sink. By the time she came back to the table, Ma had another slice of bread and jam waiting for her. Esther ate as fast as she could, impatient for the promised buggy ride.

"Change into your best dresses," Ma instructed Esther and Violet. She was already wearing her best dress—the lilac one with white flowers. She smelled faintly of lilacs, too. That meant she was wearing the dusting powder Julia had given her for Christmas. She used it only on special occasions.

"Mmmm. You smell good," Esther said. She watched Ma and hoped for a smile.

But Ma was fixing Walter's bow tie and didn't look up. "If you are finished eating, hurry and get ready," she said.

Esther bit her lip, but she supposed she mustn't expect Ma to change overnight. There was the buggy ride to enjoy, though.

She dashed upstairs. "Imagine riding a buggy to church!" she said. Even Violet admitted it would be fun. But Esther corrected her. "It will be an *adventure*—a buggy ride to a new church in a new town. Wait until I tell Julia!"

Pa came in the kitchen door just as the girls came running downstairs. They were wearing their best dresses and had matching ribbons in their hair. Pa grinned and made a deep bow. *"Guten Morgen, frauleins,"* he said. In German that meant "good morning, young ladies," so Pa was saying they looked grown up. Esther stood extra tall and grinned.

Then Pa told Ma, "The buggy is waiting." He offered her his arm.

Ma looked at him for a long moment and Esther held her breath. Was Ma still angry? Was she going to go on and on being angry the whole time they lived on the farm? But then Ma took Pa's arm and gave him a small smile. "We are ready," she said. Esther breathed again. It was all right.

Walter squealed and darted out the door. Esther wanted to race after him. But she knew she would only earn a scolding if she did. She was older and a girl. She had to act ladylike and follow Ma and Pa with Violet. She had to wait, wait, wait for everyone else to climb into the buggy before it was her turn. But finally she was sitting in the back next to Violet. They didn't even have to share the wide seat with Walter. Ma kept him up front, afraid he'd tumble out in his excitement.

Esther thought the buggy was more splendid than Shirley's Studebaker. So what if there were some tiny holes in the black leather seats? They were covered up as soon as people sat down. The main thing was it was theirs, really, truly theirs—the buggy, the horses, the land, even the shabby little house.

Unexpected pride swelled Esther's thin chest. The feeling grew and grew. If she hadn't been in the buggy, she would have let out a whoop or turned a cartwheel. Instead, she swung her legs back and forth with all her might.

The town of Johannsen's Corners was a little more than a mile and a half from the farm. Along the way, they passed other farms. Esther squinted to see if there were any girls her own age to be seen. But except for a barking dog or two, the farmyards were empty.

"Everybody's probably at church," Violet whispered anxiously. "I bet we're late."

Much to Esther's distress, it seemed Violet was right. The churchyard was nearly filled with buggies and cars when they arrived, but there were no people in sight. Ma and Pa exchanged glances. Pa's face was a question mark. Ma hesitated. Then she squared her shoulders. "We have come this far," she said.

Suddenly Esther felt shy. Bad enough to meet a bunch of new people all at once, but to walk in late and be stared at! Her stomach twisted up tight just thinking about it. Her knees trembled as she climbed down from the buggy. Then she heard the sound of another buggy rolling up. She turned just as the driver waved and called, "Welcome!"

"I'm Fredrick Klause," he said when he'd halted his horses. Then he introduced them to his wife and their two daughters. Rose was younger than Walter. Bethany looked near Esther's age.

Esther's heart gave a little skip when Bethany smiled at her. Was this girl with the dimples and dark ringlets going to be her friend—maybe even a best friend like Shirley had been? Esther smiled back. Bethany bounced down from the buggy and came right to her side.

"We missed Sunday school this morning," Bethany told Esther. She brushed a stray lock of hair back from her face, revealing a mole the size and shape of a bean on one cheek. It was brown and looked just like velvet. Esther wanted more than anything to touch it. She wanted to see if it felt as soft as it looked. But soon she was so interested in listening to Bethany that she forgot all about the mole.

"Rose hid her shoes for a joke," Bethany explained. "We looked and looked, but we couldn't find them anywhere."

"I'll bet your folks were mad," Esther said sympathetically. She knew Ma would be if Walter did such a thing.

But Bethany just laughed. "Oh, no," she said. "They thought it was funny—especially when Mama finally found the shoes in the oven!"

Esther felt her eyes bulge. In the oven! She sputtered with laughter. Ma gave her a sharp look. They were on the church steps, after all. Esther smothered her laughter and ducked her head. But she glanced sideways at Bethany's merry face and grinned.

The grown-ups' prayer group and the children's

Sunday school classes had just finished. Boys and girls were spilling in through the vestry door. Parents were herding them into pews. In all the bustle there was not so much staring as Esther had feared. There were a great many smiles and friendly greetings, though. And later, when services were ending, Reverend Phillips made a special point of welcoming them.

"We are a small community," he said, "but a close-knit one. If there is anything any of us can do to make your settling in easier, please don't hesitate to ask. We hope you'll soon feel very much at home here."

Pa and Ma nodded and smiled. Violet did, too. Esther tried, but seeing all those strange eyes at once undid her. She ended up staring at her toes. An instant later, though, everyone stood to sing the closing hymn. It was over. They'd never be brand-new again.

Several families introduced themselves. The Nielsons came over and told them about their two sets of twin boys. "The youngest two are going on ten," Sam Nielson said. "And the other two are fifteen."

"They'd be here today," Mrs. Nielson said, "but they're clearing rocks from the field so Sam can start plowing and planting this week."

Mr. Nielson chuckled. "Rocks seem to grow better than anything else in that field."

Pa laughed. "Yes. They grow well in our fields, too."

Mr. Brummel, the sheriff, stopped by next with his

wife and three nearly grown-up daughters. And last of all Mr. and Mrs. Heggersmith, the owners of the general store, came to greet them.

"If there are any groceries you need, Mrs. Vogel, we'd be happy to open the store for you," Mr. Heggersmith offered kindly. A gold tooth gleamed when he smiled. "Silly to have to make a special trip back tomorrow when you're here today."

Ma looked tempted. "You have no plans we would be upsetting?" she asked.

"Not a one," Mrs. Heggersmith said. "You come along and get all that you need."

Esther slipped away while Ma and Pa thanked them. She hoped to see Bethany one more time. She was relieved to find her new friend waiting at the foot of the church steps. When Bethany spotted Esther, she waved and gave a little skip of excitement.

"What took you so long?" she demanded when Esther had scooted down to join her. "Papa's in a hurry to leave, but I said I couldn't go without saying good-bye."

"People kept coming to meet us," Esther said. She smiled. "I'm glad you waited."

Bethany took a backward step toward the Klause buggy. "Will you be at school tomorrow?"

"I hope so." Esther held up a hand to show her crossed fingers.

"I'll see you there," Bethany promised. "I have to go now." She waved and ran off.

Walter tugged on Esther's hand. "Ma said to come," he told her.

Esther nodded and let him lead her back to the buggy. Under her breath she sang the chorus of a song she'd heard on the radio. *"Happy days are here again, the skies above are clear again . . ."*

It was a happy song, just right for this happy, happy day.

5 Country Girl

ESTHER WAS DISAPPOINTED WHEN MA announced that school would have to wait for a few days.

"First we clean. Then we unpack. *Then* you go to school," Ma said firmly. She wrinkled her nose as she eyed the house. "You can tell it was a man without a wife who lived here. No woman would let a house get so filthy."

Esther and Violet swallowed their groans and rolled up their sleeves. They swept and scrubbed and polished until Esther was sure her arms were going to fall off. She was grateful when Pa called her to help with some of the outdoor chores. They had to be much easier than housework.

But she quickly learned that nothing about farm life was easy.

She learned, for instance, that not all hens willingly give up their eggs. Some, like the scruffy brown speckled hen, actually fought to keep them! And the two geese were even nastier than the hen. They ran at her with snapping beaks when all she wanted was to feed them. "Stupid birds," Esther told them. "You should be grateful."

"Why do we need geese anyway?" she demanded of Pa, rubbing a pinched thigh tenderly. "We don't eat their eggs."

"But look," Pa said, picking up a fluffy feather from the ground. "Ma will use their feathers to make soft pillows and warm quilts. This is good, yes?"

Esther just sighed.

Feeding the pigs was not scary like collecting the eggs or feeding the geese. The little piglets tumbling and grunting in the straw were even kind of cute. But the smell in their pen was disgusting. Esther learned to take a deep, deep breath before she opened the door of the pig shed. She held her breath all the while she poured the pail of slop into their trough. She tried not to breathe until the pail was empty and she was safely outside again. But sometimes she ran out of air—ugh!

She would much rather have fed Fritz and Bruno, the

horses. Bruno, especially, was her pet. He already recognized her and nickered whenever she came into the
barn. She'd even gotten to ride him for a few minutes
with Pa looking on. Bruno's back was so wide, she had to
hang tight to his mane and hug hard with her short legs
or she would have slid right off. But oh, it was glorious to
be on a horse at last.

Esther would also have gladly fed and milked the
cows—Daisy, Buttercup, Rose, and Petunia. They were
sweet-natured, slow-moving creatures with mournful
eyes. They didn't fight to keep their milk or bite when
they were being fed.

But Pa took care of the barn animals himself. They
were too important to trust to anyone else. Without the
horses he couldn't plant or harvest crops. He couldn't get
to town for supplies. Without the cows they'd have no
milk to sell or to drink. The barn animals and the barn
that sheltered them had to be kept safe from all harm.
That's why when Esther went to tell Pa dinner was ready
that very first Sunday after church, she'd found him on a
ladder in the barn doorway.

"What are you doing, Pa?" Esther had called up to him.

Pa looked down at her. "Hanging this." He held up a
horseshoe. It was so new, it sparkled in the sunlight that
poured through the haymow window.

"But why?" Esther asked, craning her neck to see
better.

"For protection, *Liebling*," Pa explained. "And for good luck." He pulled a hammer from his belt and tapped in first one nail and then another. Then he hung the two ends of the shoe between them so it made a U.

"Isn't that upside down?" Esther called up to him.

Pa rubbed his thumb over one tip of the horseshoe before he started down the ladder. "No, it's just right," he assured Esther. "The good luck stays in the shoe instead of spilling out like it would if it were hung the other way."

Esther sucked in her breath. "How do you learn these things?"

"My pa told me, just like his pa told him." Pa had both feet on the ground again. He smiled at Esther. "Just like I am telling you." He rubbed the end of her nose with his thumb—the same thumb he'd rubbed on the end of the horseshoe. "There. Some good luck for you."

"Thanks, Pa!" Esther gasped. She was so excited, she almost forgot to tell him about dinner.

From that moment on, she had been waiting impatiently to see what kind of good luck was going to come her way.

That had been days ago, though, and nothing very nice had happened yet. In fact, that very morning had started out with Violet breaking the little mirror Julia had given her. Seven years' bad luck! And if bad luck came to Violet, who was never far from Esther's side, how likely was poor Esther to escape it?

Then Grumpy the goose had nipped her leg not once but twice! Esther didn't say anything to Pa because she didn't want to hurt his feelings, but she was beginning to doubt the power of his lucky horseshoe.

She was limping back to the farmhouse when she suddenly halted. Surely she had just seen a dog disappear around the side of the house! Heart pounding faster, she stood still as a fence post, watching. A few moments later, a white-and-orange head peeked around the porch.

Esther wanted to jump up and down. She wanted to shriek for everyone to come see what she had found. But the dog was already frightened. She couldn't risk scaring him away. She forced herself to be still, and she extended one hand invitingly. "Here, boy," she called softly. She didn't know if the dog was a boy or a girl, but she had to call it something.

The dog took a few cautious steps toward her. He had a white and rust-colored coat, a long pointy nose, and ears that stood straight up except at the very tips. His plumed tail swished shyly back and forth.

"Good boy," Esther encouraged him. "Come on." She squatted down and made a clucking noise with her tongue. "Come, boy."

The dog inched closer, tail still slowly swishing but head lowered uncertainly.

"It's all right," Esther reassured the dog. "I won't hurt you."

He couldn't have understood the words, but he seemed to understand the feeling behind them. The dog came the rest of the way to Esther. He thrust his muzzle into her outstretched hand and licked it. Esther was so thrilled, her heart nearly stopped.

"So, you have found a friend." Pa's voice came soft behind her.

The dog raised startled eyes. Esther threw her arms around him so he wouldn't run away. "I can keep him, Pa, can't I? Please. Please!"

Slowly Pa came and squatted at Esther's side. He frowned. "Dobbs never told me he was leaving him. I hired the neighbor boy to feed the animals until we came. But I never said anything to him about a dog. He must be hungry."

Esther hugged the dog closer. Suddenly, beneath his shaggy coat, she felt ribs poking up under his skin. Horrified, she leaped to her feet. "We have to feed him fast, Pa! He's starving!"

"Easy, *Liebling*," Pa said, laying a hand on Esther's shoulder. "You will frighten him." He stood up. "Wait here. I will be right back."

Esther watched impatiently as Pa strode into the house. She knelt down again to encircle the dog's body with her arms. "Don't worry, boy. You'll have something to eat soon. I promise."

But a moment later, Ma appeared in the doorway.

Esther's breath caught in her throat. Ma was going to tell her to shoo the dog away! That's what she always did when Esther brought home stray dogs and cats. She probably had told Pa not to feed him, either.

Esther could imagine it plainly. *"Nu,"* she must have said, "we have no food to waste on dogs. Besides, if we feed him, he will never go away." She always said that in the city, adding, "Don't worry. He will find food somewhere." And in the city there were lots of other people to take pity on an animal. But here there was only them.

Esther tightened her hold around the dog. She watched Ma come nearer and nearer. Esther squeezed the dog so tight, he whimpered and tried to pull away. "I'm sorry," she said quickly. She loosened her grip a little and scratched behind the dog's ears to keep him still. But her eyes never left Ma. Esther's heart thudded faster still. She would die if Ma told her she could not keep this dog. She would truly die.

Ma stopped in front of Esther. She frowned and Esther went cold all over.

"Please, Ma," she burst out. "It's the country, not the city. Please say he can stay. Please!"

Ma shook her head, and Esther's last flicker of hope died. *"Nu,"* Ma said, "why do you cry?"

Esther blinked. She hadn't realized she *was* crying until Ma told her. Hastily she wiped her eyes on the back of one hand. But the other hand held tight to the dog. He was looking up at Ma, wagging his tail. He didn't know Ma did not want him. He didn't know she wanted to send him away. His brown eyes were full of trust.

"At least let me feed him," Esther begged. "I promised him food. He's really hungry, Ma, and there's nobody else, and—" Esther stopped abruptly as Ma held up one hand.

"Hush," said Ma quietly. Then she did a strange thing. She reached out and stroked the dog's head.

Esther blinked in astonishment. "But I thought you didn't like dogs." The words popped out before Esther could stop them.

Ma raised her eyebrows at Esther. "I don't like dogs in the city," she said firmly. "But on a farm it is different." She smiled as the dog licked her hand. Then she took a step backward and nodded. "He will make a good watchdog."

Ma had turned and started back to the house before Esther could believe she'd heard right. The dog could stay. He could STAY!

The screen door banged, and Pa came out carrying two beat-up tin pans. One was filled with water. The other was filled with food—a few bits of leftover bacon, chunks of bread, and oatmeal. The dog's nose quivered as he smelled the food. He whimpered.

"Can I give it to him, please, Pa?" Esther begged.

Pa handed the tins to her. The dog was so excited, he bumped Esther's arm. A chunk of bread fell. No matter.

He snatched it up, swallowed it in one gulp, and dived for the pan, now safely on the ground. In amazement, Esther watched the dog gobble up everything in just a few seconds. He licked the tin until it shined. Then he looked up as if hoping for more.

"He's still hungry, Pa," Esther cried.

But Pa shook his head. "Too much now would make him sick. You can give him more later." He patted the dog's neck. "I think Dobbs called him Mickey," he said.

It was not the name Esther would have chosen for her dog. She would have named him Prince, or King, or maybe even Rinty. But the dog's head had turned. His tail was wagging. It was plain he recognized his name. It would be mean to change it.

Esther knelt down on the ground. "You're my dog now, Mickey. What do you think of that?" she asked. Her answer was the slurp of a tongue across half her face and all of one ear. She giggled and hugged her dog tight. The horseshoe had been good luck after all. The very best good luck she'd ever had.

Esther thought she couldn't be any happier. But that night, Ma announced that Esther and Violet could go to school the next day. Esther dashed out to the yard to tell Mickey the good news and turn two cartwheels under the stars. When she came back inside a few minutes later, she saw Violet frowning into the parlor mirror.

"Will you trim my hair, please, Ma?" Violet asked. "It's

gotten all straggly." Violet was very proud of her short bob. It was the latest fashion and didn't cost a cent.

Ma was measuring the kitchen window for curtains. She glanced outside before she nodded. "The moon is right. Go get the scissors."

Esther crinkled her eyebrows. Here was another example of the moon's importance. According to Ma, hair should only be cut when the moon was "growing." This would make the hair grow in thick and healthy. Lucky for Violet, the moon was waxing now. She got her haircut. Esther didn't want a haircut, but Ma decided to trim her hair, too, since she was barbering.

Esther had to stand straight and still. She couldn't fidget at all or Ma would scold. But sometimes the falling hairs tickled. It was impossible not to squirm a little. *"Nu,"* Ma said in exasperation, "how can I cut when you dance and jiggle?"

When the haircut was finally finished, Esther fled to her room. She was startled to find Violet there crying stormily into her pillow. "Vi! What's wrong?" Esther hurried to her sister. "Are you hurt? Should I call Ma?"

"No!" Violet sobbed. "Don't call anybody. I don't want anybody to s-see me."

"Why? What's wrong?" Esther demanded.

For answer, Violet slowly raised her pink-blotched face from the pillow.

At first all Esther could see were tears. She peered

closer. "I don't see—" Then she gasped. "What happened to your eyelashes?"

Violet's face crumpled. "I c-cut them."

Esther was astonished. "But *why?*"

"So they'll g-grow back thicker and l-longer," Violet explained between sobs. "Like my hair. But I didn't know how aw-aw-awful I'd look . . ." She shook her head. "I should have known not to do it. It was a stupid thing to do after breaking a mirror this morning. I'll probably be ugly for seven years!" Violet flung herself back into her pillow, sobbing even louder than before.

Esther patted Violet's shoulder. She felt sorry for her sister, who did indeed look strange. But she couldn't help feeling a bit smug, too. *She* had beautiful eyelashes. And they would be right where they belonged on the first day of school.

The next morning, Esther bounded out of bed. She shivered in the early-morning chill. The only heat in the house came from the stove in the kitchen and the fireplace in the parlor. Very little found its way upstairs. As fast as she could, Esther dressed in the favorite of her two school dresses—the red-and-green print. Then she threw on her coat and ran out to visit the outhouse and do her chores. Mickey was her prancing shadow. He slept under the porch but scrambled out the instant he heard her footsteps.

By the time Esther came back with the eggs, Ma was poking wood into the stove. Pa was back from the barn and was washing up at the sink.

"Good morning," Esther chirped happily, setting the egg basket on the table.

"You are up early," Pa said.

"I couldn't sleep," Esther confided. "I was too excited. I hope I get a nice teacher." She crossed her fingers.

"Just behave and you will not have to worry if she is nice," said Ma.

Esther sighed. Ma didn't understand. She'd never gone to school. She'd learned how to read and write all on her own. She didn't know that a nice teacher made learning easy, even fun. But a mean teacher made it scary and hard.

Esther ducked and dodged the laundry hanging from the clothesline in the kitchen. A storm had blown up the day before, and they'd had to bring the wash inside. Most of it had dried overnight, but some had not. The damp fabric made Esther's skin crawl when it brushed against her neck.

The kitchen sink was the only sink in the old farmhouse. Violet found that a great hardship, but Esther didn't mind. She thought it was fun to pump the handle until water spurted out. She splashed the icy water on her face and scrubbed her hands with the big caramel-colored bar of Fels-Naptha laundry soap. It didn't smell good or feel soft like Ivory. But it cost much less, so Ma bought it for everyday use.

Esther scooted back upstairs and found Violet eyeing herself in the mirror. Her lower lip was thrust out, but she wasn't crying. When she heard Esther, she turned to her with a grim but determined look on her face.

"That hair ribbon is real pretty," Esther said to cheer her.

Violet said, "Thanks." Then she clumped down the stairs.

Esther quickly made her side of the bed. Then she set Margaret on top of her pillow. "I go to school today, Margaret," she said breathlessly. "I wish you could come, too. But I'll tell you all about it when I come home. Promise." She blew the doll a kiss and started downstairs, but first she patted her pocket. She wanted to make sure the quarter Julia had given her was still safe inside. That first day they would ride to and from town with Pa. He would enroll them in school in the morning. And after school he would take them to the store to buy Violet new shoes. While they were there, Esther planned to buy stamps. Then she could write her first letter to Julia. She could tell her all about Mickey, and Bruno, and school.

"Why can't we take the buggy?" Esther asked as she and Violet settled themselves on the hard wooden floor in the back of the wagon.

"I need the wagon to carry the seed I will buy in town," Pa explained.

Esther nodded. All week Pa had been plowing the empty fields, preparing the soil. Now it was time to begin planting.

Esther had been surprised when she'd first seen the school on Sunday. It was so much smaller than her school in Chicago! It looked more like a house than an elementary school. When she went inside that first morning, she was even more surprised.

A long hallway stretched straight ahead from the entrance. It had hooks on both sides for hanging coats and hats. At the end of the hallway there were two doors. The one on the left led to the classroom for grades one through four. The one on the right was for grades five through eight. Just two classrooms in the whole school!

Esther's teacher was Miss Larson. She had thick blond braids wrapped like a crown on top of her head. Her eyes were very blue and her cheeks were very pink. Esther thought she looked just like the princess in a fairy tale.

When Pa took Violet to the room across the hall, Miss Larson introduced Esther to the class. "This is Esther Vogel, children. Let's all make her feel welcome."

Esther smiled shyly as two dozen faces stared at her. But one dimpled grin stood out from the rest. Bethany! Esther felt herself grinning back, shyness forgotten.

When Miss Larson told her to take the desk just behind her friend, Esther's joy was complete.

From her seat, Esther looked at the room more closely. Many things were the same as in her city school. There were the same rows of wooden desks that connected front to back. There was the same flag mounted in the corner. There were the same pictures of Abraham Lincoln and George Washington on the wall. And there was the same blackboard behind the teacher's desk— although this one was farther away from Esther's desk, and not so easy to see.

But some things were very different. The coal stove at the front of the room was one. The water pail and dipper in the back was another. And the outhouses Esther had glimpsed outside were another. Still, it wasn't long before Esther felt at home. School—any school—was a good place to be.

Esther discovered that Miss Larson taught reading and arithmetic in the morning. One by one she called each grade to the front of the room. The children sat on the extra seats that stuck out in front of the first desk in each row. If there were more than four students in a class, the biggest boys would have to stand, because there were only four rows of desks—one for each grade. After Miss Larson taught them a lesson, she sent the students back to their seats to work on an assignment. Then the next grade went up.

Esther watched in wonder. In the city, Miss Monksburg had only one grade to teach. She had time to grade papers and prepare lessons when her students were working. But Miss Larson was teaching nearly all the time.

At lunch, Bethany introduced Esther to the other fourth-graders. Mary Knutson had beautiful long blond hair and stuttered. Pamela Shaughnessy had more freckles than anyone Esther had ever seen. And the Nielson twins, Wesley and Thomas, looked so exactly alike, Esther could hardly keep from staring.

There was no lunchroom. At noon everyone put away their books and took out the lunches they'd brought from home. They ate right at their desks. When they were finished, they hurried out to play in the school yard. Bethany had a length of clothesline the girls used as a jump rope. Together they chanted:

> *"Buster Brown, come to town,*
> *Buster Brown, turn around,*
> *Buster Brown, touch the ground,*
> *Buster Brown, get out of town!"*

It was the same jump rope song Esther and Shirley had jumped to in Chicago! When it was her turn, Esther hopped into the turning rope. In time to the song she turned around and touched the ground. Then she skipped safely out of the rope again. Jumping felt good after sitting all morning. But when Miss Larson came out and rang her handbell, Esther was quick to join the stampede up the school steps. She could feel the smile stretching across her face.

After school, Pa drove Esther and Violet to the Heggersmiths' general store. When they left, Violet was wearing her new shoes. Esther was carrying the old pair wrapped in newspaper and tied with string. They were hers now, to wear when her shoes became tight. And even though it was nearly the end of the school year, both girls had brand-new Big Chief writing tablets and pencils. Esther climbed carefully into the back of the buggy, her precious stamps safely tucked in her pocket.

At the farm, Walter ran out of the house to meet the buggy. He hoisted himself up to the front seat to ride with Pa to the barn. Esther jumped down and raced into the farmhouse. She was eager to tell Ma all about the new school.

"The teacher reads to us at the end of each day," Esther reported excitedly. "The book she's reading now is about a doll that's one hundred years old!"

Ma wrinkled her nose. "A foolish story," she declared.

"No, Ma, really! It's a wonderful story," Esther insisted.

But Ma had tired of the topic. "Let me see your shoes," she said to Violet.

Violet pranced forward to show them off in all their shiny newness. Ma leaned over to press on Violet's toe with her thumb. She grunted her approval. "There is room to grow," she said.

Ma had been sewing at her machine. Now she stood up and shook out the curtains she'd made. They were white with red roses splashed gaily over them. Luckily, Ma's sewing machine didn't need electricity to work, just Ma's foot rocking back and forth on its treadle. The movement of the treadle made the machine whir and hum. It made the needle dart up and down, flashing in and out of the fabric.

"The curtains are pretty," Violet said, touching a hem.

Ma sighed. "Maybe they will brighten the kitchen a little." She started to pull a chair away from the table but stopped suddenly. "Are those *shoes* on the table?" she asked Esther. "You know that is bad luck!"

Esther snatched the bundle from the table. "I'm sorry, Ma. I forgot. I was so excited about school . . ." Her voice dwindled away. She knew no excuse would be good enough. Not when it came to bad luck. She hung her head.

Ma knocked on the table loudly one, two, three times. Sometimes knocking on wood could undo a curse, and three was a powerful number. "What good is school if you do not learn what is important?" Ma asked. With a sigh she whisked past Esther. The chair squealed as she shoved it across the floor to the kitchen window, where she climbed onto it.

Ma took down the curtain rod that sat on two fat nails on either side of the window. She poked it through the hem at the top of the curtains. Then she stretched to set the rod back on its perch.

Esther and Violet stood back and watched. Esther hoped the pretty curtains would cheer up Ma enough so she would forgive Esther for the bad luck that might be coming. But when the curtains were barely— beautifully—in place, Ma lost her balance.

Frozen in horror, Esther watched as Ma teetered on the chair, arms waving wildly. She grabbed desperately for something to stop herself from falling. But all she caught hold of were the curtains. The rod came loose. For a moment the curtains were like a brave flag Ma was waving. Then she screamed.

Esther blinked. She gasped. Her feet finally moved. She ran with Violet to help Ma. But they were too late. Ma crashed to the floor with the curtains still clutched in her hand.

6 Shame on Esther

April 25, 1930

Dear Julia,

A lot has happened since we arrived in Wisconsin. Most of it has been good. I have a dog named Mickey. I get to ride Bruno the workhorse. I have a best friend named Bethany. And my teacher, Miss Larson, is very nice. She is reading us a book about a doll named Hitty. It is so exciting! Even the boys like it.

But a terrible thing happened to Ma last week. She fell and hurt her ankle. It swelled up so bad, Pa thought it was broken. He took Ma to the doctor even though Ma said it was just a sprain. Turns out she was right. Now she is mad they had to pay the doctor. But it is a very bad sprain. Ma still cannot walk on it. Vi stays home from school to take care of Ma and Walter. Even though I would miss school, I wish I could stay home instead of Vi. I put shoes on the table. That is why Ma fell. I feel just awful.

Yesterday was my birthday and Vi tried to make me a cake. She put too much wood in the stove and the cake got all black. We gave it to the pigs. I didn't have a cake, so I couldn't make a birthday wish. Thanks for the pretty hair ribbons you sent. I am wearing them to school today for luck. We have a spelling bee. I want to win like I did in Chicago. The winner gets a blue ribbon here. I miss you.

Love,
Esther

Esther read her letter one last time as she walked down the rutted lane to the road. Then she folded it and slipped it into a stamped envelope with Julia's name and address in Esther's best handwriting on the front. She popped it into the battered mailbox and stood up the chipped red flag. There. Now the postman would know to stop and take her letter.

Esther bent down to pat Mickey. "Good-bye, boy. You go back and watch the house now. I'll see you after school. Go on, go home." Mickey obediently turned and trotted back up the lane. Esther watched him go. Then she set out for school.

It was a long walk, especially without Violet to talk to. Sometimes Esther met other farm children along the way. But today she didn't see anyone on the gravel road ahead, so she decided to play her favorite game—

pretend. She pretended the farmhouse was all fixed up. Outside it was painted dazzling white. The roof was new, with no ugly tar paper patches. Green shutters framed every shining window. Pots of pink geraniums and white begonias blossomed beside the door and in window boxes.

Inside, the walls were covered with pretty wallpapers—blue and yellow for the parlor, red and white for the kitchen. Crisp white curtains hung at the parlor windows. The kitchen table was covered with a white linen cloth—just like Shirley's had been—instead of red-checkered oilcloth. There was electricity and gleaming new linoleum floors. There was even a beautiful carpet in the parlor, with blue and yellow flowers all over it. Sometimes Esther pretended different colors, and sometimes she imagined a new sofa and chairs. But one thing that never changed was Ma. Esther always pretended that Ma was rocking in the pretty parlor, listening to the radio. Then Ma would see Esther. She would smile and open her arms to her . . .

A car horn beeped behind Esther. She yelped and whirled around to see her teacher parked on the side of the road. "Jump in," Miss Larson invited.

Esther could hardly believe it. Ride to school with her teacher? Such a wondrous event would never happen in Chicago. "Thank you!" she said, hopping into the automobile.

"You have a long walk," Miss Larson observed as she drove on.

Esther smiled shyly. "I don't mind. I like school."

Her teacher smiled back at her. "I can tell that by the way you listen in class, and by the careful work you do."

Esther's ears burned at this unexpected praise.

"I was wondering," Miss Larson continued, "if you might be interested in doing some teaching."

Esther was stunned. "Me?" She could hardly believe it. To be a teacher someday had long been her secret dream. But it had seemed far away and impossible. Could she really be a teacher now?

"I could use someone to help with the youngest children," Miss Larson said, shifting her gaze from the road to Esther for a moment. "Would you like to do that?"

Esther sucked in her breath. "Yes. I would like to very much!"

"You can begin on Monday," her teacher promised.

Somehow Esther contained her excitement until they reached the school. But the moment she got out of the car, she took a joyful leap into the air. She was going to teach! Esther wanted to share her news with Bethany, but Bethany wasn't in the school yard yet. She still hadn't arrived when the bell rang.

That's when Esther knew she was in trouble.

On Fridays they had an arithmetic test. Miss Larson wrote all the problems on the blackboard. But Esther couldn't see the board well from her seat. Last week Bethany had copied the problems for her before she started her own work. But Bethany was absent.

Esther entered the little schoolhouse with a sinking heart. She slid behind her desk and looked desperately at the blurry white marks on the blackboard. But they were impossible to read.

Miss Larson led the class in the Pledge of Allegiance and then told them to begin their tests.

Esther's hands began to sweat. Everyone else was hard at work copying problems. Esther squinted and squinted, but the chalk marks on the board remained fuzzy white squiggles. They hardly looked like numbers at all. The minute hand of the clock on the wall had never clicked so loudly before. One minute after another was slipping away. Soon Miss Larson would say "pencils down, class" and collect their papers. What would she think when she saw Esther's blank sheet? Tears prickled her eyes. There had to be something she could do!

Then she felt her seat shift as Wesley leaned heavily forward on the desk behind her. Wesley! Why hadn't she thought of him before? Quickly she scribbled him a note and dropped it over her shoulder onto his desk: *Wes— will you please copy the problems for me? I can't see them. Esther.*

A minute later she felt a tap on her back. She reached behind her and grabbed the folded square of paper. It said: *Yes. If you give me the answers to the fractions. Wes.*

Esther hesitated. It would be wrong to give answers to Wes. But he would lose time helping her. And there were probably only a few fraction problems on the test. Esther squirmed in her seat. She knew she was making excuses, but if she failed her test, Miss Larson probably wouldn't want Esther to help teach!

Another loud click of the clock's minute hand made up her mind. Esther signaled her agreement to the plan. The problems were copied and solved. And the answers to the fractions were passed back to Wes. A minute later, Miss Larson said, "Put your pencils down, class."

Esther heaved a big sigh. She'd finished just in time.

All was well, or so Esther thought, until Miss Larson called Wesley and Esther to her desk two hours later.

"I want to know who copied from whom on the arithmetic test," she said. Her beautiful face was one deep frown. Her eyes were not warm and friendly as they usually were. She was angry—and at Esther, who had never, ever made a teacher angry before!

Esther's knees wobbled. Her voice came out a shaky croak. "I-it wasn't like that, Miss Larson—at least, not exactly," she tried to explain. "I can't see the blackboard. So Wes copied the problems for me. And to th-thank him I gave him the answers to the fractions. That's all." She was hopeful the explanation would redeem her in her teacher's eyes. After all, she hadn't *gotten* any answers, she'd only *given* them.

But Miss Larson did not seem any better pleased. "Cheating is cheating, no matter if you're giving the answers or receiving them. I'm very disappointed in both of you. You will each get a zero on the test and you will stand at the front of the class for the fifteen minutes until lunch. And Esther, next time you ask someone to copy something for you, make certain their eyes are better than yours. Wesley copied three different problems wrong. It was when you both had the same mistakes that I knew something wasn't right."

Wesley gave Esther a lopsided grin she knew he meant to be an apology. But Esther could not grin back. She was clenching her teeth together to keep from crying. Her throat felt like it would burst with trying to keep back sobs. And her face and ears were blazing hot while the rest of her was cold as ice. She didn't know how that could be, but it was.

The other students tried to be kind. They didn't stare, except for the very youngest ones. But Esther had never been so ashamed.

At lunchtime she tried to eat but she couldn't. Her throat was still too tight. And when Mary and Pamela invited her to play tag, she shook her head. "I don't feel well," she said, and it wasn't a fib.

When they left, she pretended to read, but really she was imagining she was in her bedroom holding Margaret close. She had disappointed Miss Larson, her beautiful, kind teacher. She would never let Esther help teach now.

When the afternoon bell rang, Esther remembered the spelling bee. Suddenly it was more important than ever that she win. Before, she had just wanted the blue ribbon to make Ma proud of her, but now winning was a way to make her teacher proud of her again, too. Esther was determined to be the last speller standing.

Social studies and science seemed to take forever that day. But at last it was time for the bee. The third- and fourth-grade girls lined up along one wall. The boys lined up across the room. At their head was Thomas Nielson. Thomas was a better student than his twin, and Esther had heard he was a star speller. He wore such a cocky grin that Esther's mouth went dry. Her voice squeaked when she spelled her first word. But she spelled it correctly. That was what mattered. The next time her voice didn't squeak.

One by one, girls and boys missed words and went back to their seats. Finally, only Thomas and Esther were left. His cocky grin was gone. He frowned in concentration when Miss Larson gave him his word. For the first time he looked worried.

"Nuisance," he repeated. "N-u . . . s-a-n-c-e. Nuisance."

"That is incorrect," Miss Larson said. "Esther, can you spell *nuisance?"*

Esther's heart, already beating fast, drummed harder

and faster still. She took a deep breath. She crossed her fingers in the folds of her skirt. *"Nuisance,"* she said. "N-u-i-s-a-n-c-e." She held her breath and looked at Miss Larson.

The teacher beamed back at her. "Correct!" she announced. Excited murmurs came from the girls.

Now there was just one more word for Esther to spell. If she spelled it correctly, she would win the bee. If not, Thomas got another chance and the bee continued. Esther held her breath, waiting for the word.

"Your next word is *performance*, Esther." A hush fell over the room.

Esther let out her breath. She smiled. *"Performance.* P-e-r-f-o-r-m-a-n-c-e."

"Correct!" Miss Larson said. "Esther Vogel wins the bee." All the girls clapped.

Joyfully, Esther accepted the blue ribbon from her teacher. The scalloped paper circle pinned to the top said *Champion Speller.* Wait until Ma saw it! And Miss Larson was smiling at her. Perhaps in time she'd forget that Esther had cheated. Perhaps she'd even give her another chance to teach the first-graders. For now, though, Esther was happy just to see her teacher's smile and know that Miss Larson wasn't angry at her anymore.

But at the end of the day Miss Larson handed Esther an envelope. She handed another one to Wesley. "Please give these notes to your parents," she said. Esther felt like someone was squeezing her tight around her middle, so tight that she could barely breathe. Because she knew the note was to tell Ma and Pa she had cheated.

She whispered, "Yes, Miss Larson," with the last bit of breath in her.

After Miss Larson walked away, Wes said, "Uh-oh." Esther couldn't bring herself to look at him, though. Her own fear and misery were enough to bear. Instead, she plodded toward the door on feet that felt like they did the time she'd stepped in wet cement in Chicago. And just like that time, her feet got harder and harder to lift the closer she got to home.

Mickey ran up to meet her with a wagging tail, but Esther could only pat his head. She could not get any words out. If she tried, she was sure she would burst into tears. And if she walked into the farmhouse crying, it would just make everything worse.

If only Esther could see the blackboard like everyone else. Pa and Ma were going to be so ashamed of her! Ma would never hug Esther or tell her that she loved her now. Esther had ruined everything by cheating.

She stopped at the foot of the porch steps and took the envelope out of her reader. *Mr. and Mrs. Vogel* was written in Miss Larson's beautiful penmanship across the front. Esther bit her lip. She knew she had to give the letter to Ma and Pa. But she didn't have to give it to them right away, did she? She could wait until Sunday night. That way she could still have the joy of showing Ma and Pa her blue ribbon. And she would have the weekend for storing up memories of when they were proud of her.

She swallowed. It was cowardly, she supposed. But it was the only way she could bring herself to go inside. She shoved the envelope back into her book.

Ma was knitting in the parlor when Esther walked in. Esther pulled out her blue ribbon and waved it in the air. "Look what I've got!" she said.

Ma stopped her knitting and looked. She nodded and smiled. "Very good," she said. Then she started knitting again.

Tears stung Esther's eyes. That was all Ma had to say? Didn't she know what a good speller someone had to be to win a blue ribbon? Well, Violet would know. Her excitement would tell Ma how special the award was.

"Look, Vi," Esther said, thrusting the ribbon in front of her sister. "Isn't it splendid?"

But Violet was hunched over the sewing machine. She barely glanced at the ribbon. "Just a minute, Es . . . Ma? How do I refill the bobbin?"

Ma stood up and limped slowly across the room. "I will show you," she said.

The two had their heads together, murmuring over the machine. They seemed to have forgotten Esther was even there.

She tried to swallow the lump in her throat. "I'm going to my room," she said. And when neither Ma nor Violet said anything, she climbed the stairs.

In her bedroom, Esther yanked her birthday ribbon out of her hair. She'd worn it for luck. Well, luck she'd had, but more bad than good. Esther buried the ribbon in her dresser drawer and slammed the drawer shut.

She thought of the wish she'd planned to make on her birthday—if Violet had not burned the cake. "I wish Ma would love me and hug me like Mrs. Rubinstein hugs Shirley," she would have wished with all her might. But she hadn't gotten to make a wish. And once Ma saw the note about Esther cheating, no wishes on earth would be powerful enough to help Esther win her love. But she still had the weekend. If school ribbons couldn't impress Ma, she would just have to think of something else.

Esther paced back and forth next to the bed. Maybe she should ask for sewing lessons. Since Violet had been staying home, Ma had taught her how to use her machine. Just the night before, Ma had told Pa what a fine seamstress Violet was becoming. She had smiled at Violet with real pride.

Esther ran back downstairs. "Ma, will you teach me to sew, like Violet?" she asked. "Please."

Ma shook her head. "You are too little," she explained. "Your feet will not reach the treadle yet. When you are older, then I will teach."

Esther trudged back upstairs. It might be years before she was big enough to sew, but all she had was two days.

Esther plunked herself onto the bed. "I have to think of something," Esther said to Margaret, taking the doll on her lap. "But what?"

That night, Esther showed Pa her ribbon. He told her it was the finest blue ribbon he had ever seen. He told her he'd never known a champion speller before, and he smiled at her proudly. Esther felt a little better. If only Ma could have been as enthusiastic as Pa.

Still, Esther was determined to impress Ma, if not with ribbons, then with hard work.

She was the first one up from the supper table that night. She carried more dishes to the sink than Ma and Violet did together, and she dried them until they squeaked. After supper she swept the kitchen floor, and when Ma didn't seem to notice, she called, "I'll just sweep off the porch, too, while I'm at it."

But when she came back inside, Ma was talking to Pa. She didn't say, "Thank you, Esther. What a fine helper you are!" She didn't look at Esther with pride glowing in her eyes. She didn't say anything at all.

Esther was tired. She went up to bed early. But alone in the darkness, all she could think of was the note from Miss Larson. She kept imagining how horrified Ma and Pa would be when they read it. She hadn't wanted to cheat. She hadn't meant to bring shame to Ma and Pa. She hugged Margaret to her chest and sobbed into her pillow.

Maybe she should have just given them the note and gotten it over with. Putting it off was only stretching out her misery. But maybe tomorrow would be different. Maybe she would be able to make Ma and Pa proud of her for at least a little while before they found out what she'd done.

The next morning, after Esther did her chores, she brought in wood to fill the basket by the stove. She set the table for breakfast and cleared it afterward. Then she dusted the furniture in the parlor without being told. She dusted the legs and the feet of the furniture, too, not just the tops. But all Ma said was, "Shake out the cloth when you are done."

Esther shook out the cloth. Then she shook out the rag rugs from the parlor and the kitchen. Her arms ached, and when she saw Bruno in the pasture, her heart ached, too. It was sunny and warm. How much fun a ride would be! But she went back into the house. She polished the parlor mirror with a soft cloth and vinegar. She tidied Pa's stack of seed catalogs. Then she looked around for some other job to do. "Ma, I think I'll wash the floor," she announced on her way to the pantry for the mop.

"*Nu*," said Ma, sounding a little annoyed. "I just waxed it yesterday. Can you not tell?"

"Oh, sure," Esther said quickly. "Of course." Although the truth was the floor was so scarred and stained that even Ma's scrubbing and waxing could not make it shiny or bright. "Is there something else I could do—to help you?" she added.

Ma frowned in thought. "I cannot think of anything," she said at last. "You have done everything already." She smiled. "You—"

The kitchen door opened and Pa called to Ma for the peroxide. He had cut his hand working in the barn. Ma hurried to help him.

Esther felt sorry for Pa. But she felt sorry for herself, too. What had Ma been about to say?

Esther looked on as Ma bathed the cut with soap and water and then with peroxide before wrapping a bandage around it. When Pa finally headed back to the barn, Esther waited expectantly. But after Ma put away the peroxide, she took out a pot and filled it with water. She put it on the stove to hard-boil some eggs. She had forgotten whatever she was going to say to Esther.

Esther went up to her room and found Margaret. "Nothing I do seems to make any difference," she told the doll. "Maybe that's because I'm not being honest. Maybe God is angry at me for not giving Ma and Pa the note right away. Do you think that could be it?" Margaret's china-blue eyes stared solemnly back at Esther. It was very clear to Esther what Margaret thought.

Esther sighed and took the envelope from her reader. She made herself stand straight and tall. Then she took the envelope downstairs to Ma. "It's a note from my teacher," she said in a small voice.

Ma looked surprised, but she didn't ask what the note was about or why Esther hadn't given it to her sooner. She just tore open the envelope and began to read. Esther, burning with shame, stared at the floor and tried not to cry. When she heard the rustle of the note being folded back into the envelope, she sneaked a quick peek at Ma's face. There were two bright spots of red on her cheeks. Esther gulped and looked back at the floor. Ma was furious.

"This fine teacher of yours," Ma said, "vill she buy these eyeglasses for you?"

Esther's head snapped up. Eyeglasses? "Wh-what do you mean, Ma?" Esther's heart did a skip and a jump. Was the letter about eyeglasses? Not cheating?

Ma tore the envelope across and then tore the pieces across one more time. "Your teacher says you cannot see vell. She says ve should buy you eyeglasses. Does she think ve are rich?" Ma sniffed. "Ve don't have money for eyeglasses. Maybe after the harvest. But not now. Your teacher should mind her own business."

"Yes, Ma," Esther said automatically. But what she was thinking was, Miss Larson had not told on her. She hadn't told! Relief made Esther want to laugh out loud. It was all right. Ma and Pa would not be ashamed of her after all. And she would never, ever cheat again.

She felt as if she could run three times around the pasture and do ten cartwheels in a row. She felt as light as a balloon that could sail away on the tiniest breeze.

Esther's happiness continued all through the rest of the weekend. And when Monday came, she was not ashamed to face her teacher again. She knew Miss Larson had forgiven her. But even so, she was amazed by what happened that morning in school.

When it was time for arithmetic, Miss Larson came to stand beside Esther's desk. "From now on, Esther, I want you and Wesley to come up front to copy from the board. Then you may go back to your seats to do the work. All right?"

Why, that would solve everything! "Yes, Miss Larson," Esther said happily.

"Yes, Miss Larson," Wesley echoed.

"Good." The teacher started to walk away but stopped and turned back only a step from Esther's desk. "Oh, and Esther, when you finish your afternoon work, you may listen to the first-graders read aloud, one at a time, in the hallway."

Esther felt her mouth fall open. "You mean I-I can still help teach?"

Miss Larson smiled. "Yes, Esther. If you want to."

If she wanted to! "Oh, yes. Yes, I do!" Esther had to grip

the edge of her desk to keep from jumping out of her seat, she was so happy and excited. Wait 'til I write to Julia, she thought. Wait 'til I tell her I won the spelling bee *and* I'm going to help teach! Won't she be surprised!

Esther touched the birthday ribbon in her hair. She had pulled it back out of her drawer right after Ma read Miss Larson's letter. It was a lucky ribbon after all!

7 A Sign of Warning

July 4, 1930

Dear Julia,

I hate summer. I miss school and my friends. Vi is no fun. Ma told her she can make her own school clothes if she practices making patterns and sewing. Now that is all she does! I asked Ma if she would show me how to make patterns for clothes for Margaret. She said I am too old for dolls. Thank goodness I have Mickey to play with. He fetches sticks and runs races with me. We even play hide-and-seek. Only I am always the one to hide and Mickey always finds me.

Ma has a big vegetable garden. I help her pull weeds. How come weeds grow so much faster than vegetables? I am sorry David lost his job. I hope he finds another one fast. It has been awful hot here. If we were in Chicago, we could go to the beach with you and David.

Your last letter reminded me of how much fun that is. The water is so cold, but it feels so good! Or maybe we could go to Riverview and ride the rides and watch the fireworks like we did last year. But here every day is the same. Even the Fourth of July.

Esther laid down her pencil. She knew her letter was one long grumble, but she couldn't help it. The last few days had been so terribly hot, it was hard to sleep at night, so everyone was cranky. Even Pa, who hardly ever scolded, snapped at Walter for singing at breakfast. But Esther suspected it was more than the heat that was making Pa edgy.

"The crops need rain," she'd heard him tell Ma two days ago.

"The rain will come. Do not worry," Ma had soothed him. But the weather had continued to be hot and sunny. There weren't even any clouds in the sky.

Esther had thought their worries would be over once they moved to the farm. Pa had a job that no one could take away from him. But in the city, if he worked, he got paid. Farmers could work and work and still not earn any money if the weather wasn't right.

In the city, Pa wasn't constantly watching the sky and he didn't worry so much about signs. Just yesterday he'd come to lunch frowning nervously. "Anna, what does it mean when you see six crows on a fence but then two more land beside them?"

Ma had stopped halfway to the table as Pa spoke. But then she came the rest of the way wearing a look of relief. "You start over again, and two is luck," she said.

Pa sagged in his chair and grinned. "Thank goodness."

"Crows?" Esther asked.

Ma nodded and began to chant:

> *"One is bad,*
> *Two is luck,*
> *Three is health,*
> *Four is wealth,*
> *Five is sickness,*
> *Six is death."*

Death! No wonder Pa had looked so nervous. If the last two crows hadn't landed beside the others . . . ! Esther felt a chill even though the day was so hot.

But good luck hadn't arrived yet that Esther could see. Just more heat and dust and a weary slump to Pa's shoulders. Esther didn't want to worry about the crops. It just made her crankier. If only there was something fun to do. She'd played with Margaret for most of the morning. And she'd tried to play with Mickey. But his tongue hung out and he panted like a tired old train, huffing and puffing. She finally sent him to his shady nest under the porch and came back into the house.

Esther eyed the two books she owned—*Little Women*

and *Heidi*—stacked neatly on top of the dresser. They were last year's Christmas gifts from Kate and Julia. She'd already read them twice, but she could read one of them a third time, she supposed. She sighed. If only there were a library in town! With new books to read, she wouldn't miss school so much. And if Bethany lived nearer, so they could see each other sometimes, she wouldn't be so lonely. She thought of how easy it had been to visit Shirley in Chicago. It was very different in the country.

Esther looked out the window. Pa was walking back from the oat field. Every day he checked the oats, the corn, the wheat, and the potatoes. Every day he drove milk and eggs to town to sell. Every day he hauled and chopped wood to build the woodpile high before winter. And he made repairs around the house and barn.

But all the while Esther could tell he was really waiting. Waiting for rain. Waiting for the crops to grow. Waiting for the harvest.

The screen door banged and Esther heard Pa shout over the jingle of the fairy bells, "Everyone get ready! We are going on a picnic!"

Esther let out a whoop. She raced down the stairs. "A picnic! Where?"

"We will go to the lake and cool off for a while," Pa was telling Ma. "Maybe I will catch some fish for supper."

Ma's flushed face broke into a smile. She'd just come

in from weeding the vegetable garden. It was hot, hard work. "I will make sandwiches," she said. "Girls, come help."

Violet sprang up from the sewing machine and hurried into the kitchen. Esther was right behind her. A picnic at the lake! And here she'd just been thinking there was nothing fun to do in the country.

Esther had heard about the little lake east of town, but she'd never seen it. "Ohhh," she breathed when Pa drove into the clearing an hour later. Blue water glittered silver under the sun. "It's beautiful!" Other wagons and buggies were parked among the trees. She heard shrieks of laughter. Then she spotted Bethany hopping up and down and waving.

"I knew you'd come!" Bethany cried when Esther jumped down from the buggy. "Just about everybody does on the Fourth." Bethany hauled Esther around blankets and baskets and small, toddling children. At the shore of the lake she tossed off her shoes and socks. "Come on!"

Laughing, Esther threw off her own shoes and socks and plunged into the chilly water after Bethany. Many of their schoolmates were already splashing and chasing one another. Esther and Bethany quickly joined in the fun. When they waded back to shore a while later, Esther had forgotten all her grumpy feelings of the morning.

"Your nose is pink," she teased Bethany.

Bethany laughed. "So's yours." She wrung water from her skirt.

"Let's go get something to eat," Esther suggested. "I'm starving."

Bethany smacked her lips. "Mama brought raspberry cobbler."

Esther's mouth watered. "Ma brought sugar cookies," she said. She laughed. "She baked them after we went to bed last night for a Fourth of July surprise. But even she didn't know about the picnic. That was Pa's surprise! And it was the best one of all."

Ma was under a maple tree not far from the Heggersmiths. She had spread an old quilt on the grass. On it was a plate of sandwiches wrapped in waxed paper, a bowl of hard-boiled eggs, and a tin that Esther knew held two dozen perfect sugar cookies. There was also a small dish of plump red raspberries.

Esther reached down and plucked a berry from the dish. "Mmmm," she said, savoring its sweet juiciness. "Where'd we get the raspberries from, Ma?"

"From Mrs. Neilson. It was kind of her. She says they have more than they can eat." Ma, always generous to guests, nodded at Bethany. "Take some. They are good."

But Bethany smiled and shook her head. "No, thank you, Mrs. Vogel. We have heaps of raspberries at home right now, too. Save them for your family."

"Where are they, anyway?" Esther asked, looking around.

"Pa and Walter are fishing. Violet is with friends," Ma said. She looked unusually content, fanning herself gently with Pa's straw hat. She raised her eyebrows at Esther's and Bethany's dripping skirts. "You two look cool enough."

Esther laughed. "The water feels so good, Ma. You should go in."

Ma smiled. "Playing in water is for children."

"Mama went in last summer, Mrs. Vogel," Bethany confided. "Of course, no one was here but us. She said it was delightfully refreshing." Bethany grinned and pulled wet hair back from her face.

"Maybe you could do that, too, sometime, Ma!" Esther cried.

Ma was smiling. She was almost laughing. She opened her mouth to reply. Then, suddenly, she stiffened. Her laugh died. Her smile vanished.

She sat up straight and dropped the straw hat. A frown creased her forehead. "You should go to your family now," she said abruptly to Bethany. Then she turned to Esther. "Go find Pa and Violet. Tell them it is time to eat."

Esther stared. What was wrong with Ma? She had practically told Bethany to go away!

"You heard me, Esther," Ma said sharply. "Go find Pa."

Bethany looked as bewildered as Esther felt. "I guess I've got to eat now," Esther told her friend. "But I'll see you after lunch."

"We are not staying," Ma cut in firmly. "Now, do as I tell you."

Confused and upset, Esther went. What had happened to Ma? She'd been so happy one minute, and almost angry the next. It didn't make any sense. Tears blurred Esther's eyes and she stumbled more than once as she searched for Pa. Surely Ma hadn't meant it when she said they weren't staying. They couldn't leave yet. They'd just arrived!

She found Pa fishing in a shady cove not far down the shore. Walter was digging with a stick nearby. "Pa, Ma sent me to tell you it's time to eat," Esther said.

Pa's forehead wrinkled. "So soon?"

"All of a sudden she's in a big hurry to eat and go home," Esther said miserably.

"I don't want to go!" Walter cried. He dangled a worm up for Pa to see. "Look, Pa, I got another one!"

"Very good, Walter. Put it in the can with the others and come. It is lunchtime." Pa pulled his line from the water and picked up two fish from the grassy bank. He patted Esther's shoulder. "I will talk to Ma."

But Pa could not change Ma's mind. Neither could the Heggersmiths and Nielsons. "I have a bad headache," she told them. Esther blinked in surprise. She hadn't known Ma wasn't feeling well.

"It's not fair," Violet said as she and Esther shook crumbs from the quilt after lunch. "Peter asked me to be his partner in the three-legged race."

"Games?" Esther wailed. "There are going to be games?"

"And fireworks," Violet added bitterly. "Mr. Heggersmith sets some off every year."

Esther wanted to sit on the ground and howl.

The ride home was a silent one. No one but Ma had wanted to leave. Now they just wanted the ride home to be over. Pa tried to whistle once, but the song trailed off before he'd gotten out more than a few notes. His heart plainly wasn't in it.

Esther could understand that easily enough. Her own misery was so keen, her chest actually hurt with the strain of holding sobs inside. She was only thankful that she had managed to slip away long enough to say good-bye to Bethany. "I'm sorry about the way Ma acted," she had apologized. "She's got a bad headache."

Good-natured Bethany waved off Esther's apology. "It's all right. But listen to the great idea I had—and Mama says it's fine with her. You can come for lunch, and after, we can pick raspberries. Our bushes are loaded." Bethany was dancing from foot to foot in excitement. "Wouldn't it be fun to have a whole afternoon together?"

Esther's spirits had risen considerably. "Yes! I'll come for sure if Ma will let me."

"Mama said to come Wednesday at noon if you can," Bethany told her.

So the plan was made. And thinking of it was all that kept Esther from crying on the hot ride home. When they got to the farmhouse, she stopped on the porch to greet Mickey. But Ma called, "Esther, come here."

Ma's voice sounded funny. Was she angry at Esther? Esther hurried inside. "Yes, Ma?"

Ma was unpacking the picnic leftovers. She barely glanced at Esther. "You will stay away from the Klause girl from now on," she said.

She said it quite plainly, so Esther knew she hadn't misunderstood. But she could not believe Ma would say such a thing.

Pa walked in carrying the two fish he had caught. Esther looked to him for help. But he shook his head. He would not go against Ma.

"B-but why, Ma?" Esther finally managed. "Why do you want me to stay away from Bethany?"

"Because she is marked," Ma said. "It is dangerous to be near her."

"Marked? Dangerous?" Esther echoed in confusion. "What do you mean?"

Ma wasn't used to being questioned. "*Nu!* The mark on her face," she said impatiently. "It is a sign."

Suddenly Esther understood. "You mean the mole on her cheek?"

"Yes!" Ma nodded vigorously.

"But I have a mole on my shoulder," Esther said. "Am I marked, too?" Her heart was beating very fast.

"No," Ma said quickly. "No. Yours is small and hidden. But hers is large and on her face for all to see and be warned."

"But marked by who, Ma?" Esther asked.

"By angry fairies." Ma walked to the doorway and swung the screen door open and closed twice to ring the fairy bells. She looked back at Esther. "It is important to keep the fairies happy."

"But why, Ma? Why would fairies do that to a little baby?"

Ma shrugged. "Who knows? As a punishment to her parents, probably."

"B-but that's not fair!" Esther cried.

"I don't know about fair," Ma said. "I only know how dangerous it is to ignore fairies. And I know that the child is cursed. To be near her is dangerous."

Esther shivered. "B-but Bethany is my f-friend."

Ma shook her head so hard, a hairpin flew from her bun and pinged onto the floor. She stooped to pick it up, and when she stood and looked at Esther, her face had closed like a curtain. "Not anymore," she said firmly. Then she turned and walked away. The conversation was over.

Stunned, hardly knowing what she was doing, Esther climbed the stairs to her bedroom. Her head was whirling. Bethany dangerous? How could that be? She was good and kind. But Ma was so sure. And Ma knew things other people didn't. She knew all about signs.

Esther paced around the tiny room. Couldn't Ma be mistaken, like she was about the Tatiana dream she'd had the night before they moved? Esther picked up the letter to Julia she had started that morning. She wrote furiously with her pencil:

We just came back from a picnic at the lake. It was so much fun. But Ma made us come home early. She saw the mole on Bethany's face. She says it is the mark of angry fairies. She says it's a warning that Bethany is dangerous, and she won't let me play with her anymore. Do you think Ma could be wrong just this once? Bethany is so nice. Can she really be dangerous like Ma says? I am so sad.

I wish you were here.

Love,
Esther

8 Disobeying Ma

JUST AS THEY WERE CLIMBING INTO THE buggy on Sunday morning, Walter clutched his stomach and moaned, "I feel sick, Ma."

Ma felt Walter's forehead. "You are cool. Probably you had too much bacon," she said with a meaningful look.

Esther could not help grinning as Walter blinked at Ma in surprise. He had taken extra bacon from the platter when Ma had not been looking. Still she had known.

"Esther, you will stay home with your brother," Ma decided.

"Can't Violet stay instead?" Esther begged. She had to see Bethany and tell her she couldn't come to her house on Wednesday.

"No," Ma said. "Violet missed school when I hurt my ankle. Now it is your turn."

Esther sighed and went back inside. She put Walter to bed and changed out of her good dress. Then she told Walter a story—a made-up story—all about a brave prince who lost his kingdom. He had to fight lots of battles to win it back. He fought an evil knight. He outwitted a wicked witch. And he battled a ferocious, fire-breathing dragon. By the end of the story, Walter's eyes were closing. Esther tiptoed out of his room.

Downstairs, Esther sat at the table with her chin in her palm. What should she do? Bethany would be expecting her on Wednesday. She'd wait and wait. Too late, Esther realized she should have asked Violet to tell Bethany. But things had happened so quickly! If only Walter hadn't gotten sick. Then, during their Sunday school class, when they were away from the grown-ups, Esther could have told Bethany she couldn't come. Of course, then she would've also had to tell her why.

Esther groaned. How could she tell Bethany Ma said she was marked by evil fairies and dangerous? Bethany would be so hurt!

But Esther had to tell her something. Maybe she should go on Wednesday after all. Then she and Bethany could have one last special day together. And when it was time to leave, she could explain everything to her. But going would mean disobeying Ma.

All day Esther wrestled with the problem, but she came no closer to finding an answer. First she'd decide she would go see her friend. Then she'd remind herself that would mean disobeying Ma, and she'd resolve to stay home. Then she'd think of how Bethany would be expecting her, and she'd decide to go all over again. Back and forth. Back and forth. She wished she had someone to ask for advice. But Julia was too far away. And Esther already knew that Violet would tell her to stay home.

Violet had been very sympathetic when Esther told her Ma wouldn't let her play with Bethany anymore. "You mean *that's* why we had to come home early from the lake?" She had rolled her eyes. "You've been around Bethany for weeks and nothing awful has happened." But Violet's sympathy was one thing. Expecting her to approve of Esther sneaking off to see her friend was another thing entirely.

Late in the afternoon, Esther was playing on the porch with Mickey. Suddenly she felt a sharp pain in her foot. "Ouch!" she yelped. She hobbled into the house. "Ma, I've got a sliver."

Ma was at the stove stirring a pot of stew. She looked at Esther and raised her eyebrows. "I told you not to go barefoot."

Esther ducked her head. "I'm sorry. But it's so hot, and I was just on the porch."

Ma set down her spoon and took the first aid basket from the cupboard. She slid a chair over to Esther. "Sit," she said. Then Ma knelt on the floor in front of the chair. She lifted Esther's foot to the light from the window. "Ah," she murmured.

"Is it bad?" Esther asked anxiously.

Ma shook her head. "Not so bad. I can get it. Just be still."

Esther gripped the sides of the chair tightly. She held her breath as Ma squeezed on either side of the splinter to push it out as far as it would go. *O-ooh!* Esther bit her lip to keep from crying out. Then Ma said, "There!" and the pain was gone.

"It's out?" Esther asked.

Ma held up her tweezers so Esther could see the tiny shaft of wood.

Esther sagged in relief. She knew she had been lucky. If the splinter had been buried deep, Ma would have had to pick it out with a needle. That would have hurt a lot more. But either way, getting the splinter out hurt less than leaving it in. "Thanks, Ma," she said.

But Ma wasn't finished yet. First she swabbed the wound thoroughly with peroxide. That stung a bit, but Esther liked watching the bubbles it made. When the peroxide stopped making bubbles, Ma patted Esther's foot dry, put a small bandage on it, and stood up. "Next time, do as you are told," Ma said. "Then you will not get hurt."

"Did you always obey when you were a girl, Ma?" Esther asked, pushing the chair back to the table.

"Yes," Ma said firmly. She opened her mouth as if she wanted to say more but wasn't sure if she should. In a few moments she added, "But my little sister Tatiana did not. She was always laughing and imagining things—like you. She did not always take rules seriously." Ma's voice was suddenly so soft, Esther could barely hear her. Tatiana again! Esther wondered why Ma had never spoken of this sister before.

"Is Aunt Tatiana still in Russia?" she asked. Esther knew she had aunts and uncles in Canada. They sent letters and cards sometimes. There was Aunt Marta and Aunt Sophia, and Uncle Walter. But no Aunt Tatiana. If she still lived in Russia, that might be why she was mentioned so seldom.

"She is in Russia, yes," Ma said, but her voice sounded funny.

"Maybe she can come to visit us sometime," Esther said.

One corner of Ma's mouth quirked into a sad smile. "No, Esther. She cannot come to visit."

Esther frowned. "But why not? Uncle Josef came once."

Ma sighed. She rested one hand gently on Esther's shoulder. "Tatiana was willful. She had been told many times to stay away from the stream that went through our land. The current could be very strong, especially in the spring. But one day when she was five years old, Tatiana went in wading anyway, and she drowned."

"Oh! That's terrible!" Esther cried.

"Yes," Ma agreed. "And it wouldn't have happened if she had not disobeyed."

Esther gulped. Right then she made up her mind to stay home on Wednesday. Ma knew best. And it would be wrong to disobey her.

When Wednesday morning came, though, Esther began to have second thoughts. She imagined Bethany getting ready for her visit. She imagined her watching and waiting when it got near lunchtime. And she imagined how disappointed she would be when Esther never came. Then she remembered how Bethany had copied problems from the blackboard for her. She remembered how Bethany had waited for her on the day of the picnic. She hadn't even wet her toes in the water until Esther arrived.

Truly, Bethany was a good friend. Her best friend. And Esther felt in her heart that this one time Ma was wrong. It was just an ordinary mole on Bethany's cheek, not a mark of warning. Esther hated to disobey Ma. But she decided she had no choice.

"Ma, I finished all the lamps. Is it all right if I go pick some raspberries?" It was midmorning. Esther had spent the past hour polishing the kerosene lamps. It was a chore she hated because the smoky smudges on the glass were so stubborn. She had to rub and rub until her shoulders ached. But the last lamp was gleaming on the kitchen table. Now was the time to try her plan. She crossed two sets of fingers behind her back.

Ma was washing clothes in the yard. She used two washtubs for the job. One had soapy water in it for the washing. The other tub had clear water for the rinsing. Somewhere in the middle of the wash, Ma would empty both tubs into the grass. Then she would carry buckets of hot water from the kitchen and cold water from the well until both tubs were filled with clean water again. The buckets were too heavy for Esther to carry, but Ma was strong. And even though washing clothes was much harder here than it had been in the city, she never complained.

Ma was on her knees scrubbing one of Pa's shirts on the gray rippled washboard. Sweat streamed down her face. Hearing Esther's question, she stopped and wiped her forehead on her arm. "Raspberries and cream would be a good treat," she admitted. "You know where these berries grow?"

"Yes, and I'll bring home lots," Esther promised. She held her breath.

Ma smiled. "Go, then. There are buckets in the barn. Too bad I need Violet to help me or she could pick, too." She looked across the yard to where Violet was hanging wet clothes on the line. It was a chore Esther couldn't help with yet because she was too short.

"Thanks, Ma." Esther ran for the buckets.

A few minutes later Esther was on her way. Ma had wrapped a sandwich in waxed paper and set it inside one of the buckets. "You will get hungry," she told Esther. Then she nested that bucket inside the other one. "There," she said when she was finished. "Now they both have something in them," she explained. "To carry an empty bucket is bad luck."

Esther didn't know how Ma kept track of so many ways to avoid bad luck, but she took the buckets and said, "Thanks, Ma. I'll bring home lots of berries."

On her way to the road, feeling guiltier than ever, she fed the sandwich to Mickey so it would not go to waste. Then she put the crumpled sheet of waxed paper back in the bucket so it wouldn't be empty. She spotted Pa walking through the wheat field. Still no rain had come. Pa's walk was slow.

Walter skipped behind him, raising little clouds of dust. Esther looked up at the sky. There were a few clouds off in the distance. Please, please, rain here, she begged them silently.

It was a long walk to Bethany's house. It was even farther away than the school. To make the walk more interesting, Esther pretended she was a brave explorer alone in the jungle. The cows in the fields were elephants.

The horses were giraffes. And the dogs and cats in the farmyards were lions and tigers. She skulked past mailboxes on silent feet—the lions and tigers mustn't hear! She trotted along the fence line with one spirited giraffe. And she made monkey noises at the elephants. They twitched their ears and one or two turned to stare.

Esther laughed and chattered and loped along, swinging her buckets. In a surprisingly short time she was turning off the road at Bethany's farm. And Bethany must have been watching, because she came running to meet her.

Suddenly Esther remembered what Ma had said: "She is marked to warn people that she is dangerous." An icy shiver trickled down her spine.

"You came!" Bethany cried.

Her grin was enormous. Its warmth melted Esther's fear in an instant. "Of course I came," she said.

Esther grabbed Bethany's outstretched hand. They ran the rest of the way to the house. The closer they got, the more astonished Esther became. She had never seen Bethany's house close up before. She'd only seen it from the road, and trees had partly blocked it. Now she could see it was white with green shutters. It had pots of geraniums on the porch, and even a rocking chair. It was just like her dream house, only bigger and better. She didn't realize she had stopped to stare until Bethany tugged on her hand.

"Come on," Bethany urged. "Mama's waiting."

Dazed, Esther tripped up the porch steps after her friend. Inside the house, she tried not to gawk. She had expected Bethany's home to be much like her own. But it was far more like Shirley's pretty home in Chicago than the Vogel farmhouse. There were carpets on the floors and pretty wallpapers on the walls. There were vases of flowers on the tables and snowy-white lace curtains at the window. And nowhere was there even one nasty old kerosene lamp. They had electricity.

"Hello, Esther," Mrs. Klause greeted her from the kitchen—a kitchen with a real sink, a coal stove, and an icebox. "I hope you like pancakes, fried apples, and sausages."

Esther's mouth watered. "I love them!" she said.

Lunch was delicious, but more than that, it was fun. Lunch for the Klause family was not just a time to eat. It was a time to talk and share and laugh together. Mr. Klause especially never seemed to run out of interesting stories to tell.

"Old Brownie got a real close look at a rabbit today," he said with a grin. "He nearly put his hoof right on the fool thing before it woke up!"

Little Rose's eyes widened. "Did the bunny hop away, Papa? Did he?"

"You just bet he did, Rosy-Posy. You just bet he did,"

Mr. Klause assured her. "But that silly old Brownie gave the biggest hop of all. That's how scared he was of that little bitty bunny."

Esther laughed along with everyone else, picturing the big workhorse leaping into the air like an enormous rabbit.

Later, when the meal was nearly finished, Mr. Klause turned a suddenly serious face on Bethany and Esther. "Just be sure to put more raspberries in your pails than in your stomachs," he warned.

Esther sat up straighter and nodded. She didn't realize Mr. Klause was teasing until she heard Bethany's unladylike snort. Bethany pointed a finger at her father. "You're the one who eats as fast as he picks!"

"He surely does," Mrs. Klause agreed. "If I left the picking to him, the rest of us would never see a berry." But she smiled at her husband. And Esther noticed that Mrs. Klause gave him an extra-big serving of raspberry pie for dessert.

Everyone laughed when Rose licked her dessert plate and got a raspberry stain on her nose. Mrs. Klause kissed Rose's chubby cheek and said, "Now you are for certain the sweetest baby in Wisconsin!"

Watching Mrs. Klause with Rose, Esther felt an actual ache in her heart. Had Ma ever kissed Esther like that? She did not think so.

Esther started to clear the table, but Mrs. Klause shooed her away. "This is your holiday. You girls go and play. I can manage."

So Esther and Bethany went outside and, swinging their buckets, headed toward the raspberry bushes. They hadn't gone very far when a black cat streaked across the grass in front of them. "A black cat!" Esther gasped, plowing to a stop. "Where did he come from?"

"From our barn," Bethany said with a laugh. "Dad says Licorice is the best mouser we've ever had."

Both girls watched as the cat slowed and flattened himself in the grass. He crept forward, closer and closer to something in the grass that only he could see. Esther turned away when the cat pounced.

"Doesn't your father worry about bad luck?" she asked Bethany.

"Nah. He's just happy to have a barn with no mice."

Esther couldn't believe how calm Bethany was. Didn't she realize that bad luck was heading toward them, ready to pounce like Licorice had just pounced on that poor little creature in the grass? Esther grabbed Bethany's arm. "Come on," she said. "We have to undo our bad luck—fast!"

Bethany looked startled, but when Esther bolted for the barn, she followed. Only after they plunged into its cool shadows did Esther stop. She blinked until her eyes adjusted to the dim light. Then she scanned the walls.

"What are you looking for?" Bethany wanted to know.

"This!" Esther announced triumphantly. She set down her buckets and darted over to a low shelf where several horseshoes lay. Esther grasped a cool, heavy shoe in one hand and rubbed its ends hard with the other. Then she insisted that Bethany do the same. "There," she said, setting the shoe down again after Bethany had obeyed. "Now we're protected."

"But from what?" Bethany asked.

"From whatever bad luck your black cat was going to send us," Esther explained.

"I don't think Licorice has ever sent anyone bad luck," Bethany said doubtfully, "but I guess it can't hurt to be careful." She picked up the buckets Esther had dropped moments before. "Can we go pick raspberries now?"

Esther grinned. "We sure can." She gave a little skip into the doorway. "Heaps and heaps of raspberries." She was proud of herself for remembering what Pa had taught her that first week on the farm. For one horrible moment after she had seen the black cat, she had thought that maybe bad luck was meant to be her punishment for disobeying Ma. But because Esther had remembered Pa's lesson, she had chased the bad luck away. Of course, Pa had said the tips of the horseshoe had to be hung pointing up so the good luck didn't fall out. The horseshoe she had found was lying on its side. Maybe the good luck in it wasn't as strong as it should have been . . .

But as quickly as the worry blossomed, Esther cast it away. Even if a teeny bit of luck had spilled out, much more must have stayed inside. And a few minutes later, when she was filling her pails with raspberry after plump raspberry, she was sure of it. This was a perfect day and not even a black cat was going to spoil it.

The girls had a lot to talk about, and the faster they talked, the faster they picked.

"Were there really games at the lake?" Esther asked.

"Yes," Bethany said. "I'm sorry you couldn't stay. I wanted you for my partner."

"That would've been *so* much fun," Esther said, not even trying to keep the disappointment out of her voice.

"We'll do it next year," Bethany said, waving off a fat bee that buzzed around their heads.

Esther thought of Ma and squirmed, but she said, "Yes. Next year for sure."

When their buckets were full, the girls turned cartwheels and tried to do handstands, but the grass was dry and prickly. The sun was hot and the bees kept buzzing overhead. Esther knew they only wanted the berries, but she couldn't help being nervous. Bugs—especially bugs that stung—still frightened her a little, even after her months on the farm. She was glad when Bethany said she was thirsty and suggested they go back to the house.

Mrs. Klause poured them each a tall glass of lemonade. Esther drained the glass, one tangy mouthful after another. She had never tasted lemonade so good. But everything about that day seemed special. She wished it never had to end.

"This is so pretty," she said when Bethany took her up to her bedroom. Blue flowered wallpaper, white lace curtains, and a blue-and-white quilt made the room bright and cozy. A small white bookcase stood against one wall. Esther hurried over. "Oh! You have *Five Little Peppers*," she cried. "I loved that story. And you've got all of Louisa May Alcott's books, too!"

Bethany nodded. "Mama got them for me. I haven't read most of them yet."

Esther was shocked. "Why not? I'd be reading 'til my eyes crossed." She opened *Jo's Boys*. On the inside of the cover there was flowing handwriting that read, *To My Dear Bethany With Much Love From Mama*. Esther swallowed hard.

"You can take it home and read it if you want," Bethany offered.

But Esther put the book back on the shelf and shook her head. "No, I couldn't. I might get it dirty or lose it or something."

"You wouldn't," Bethany argued.

But Esther didn't give in, much as she would have loved to. "I really can't. But thanks," she said. She couldn't tell Bethany that there'd be no way to explain the borrowed book to Ma.

And, she realized with a pang of distress, she couldn't tell Bethany they couldn't be friends anymore, either.

She thought she'd find a way, but being with Bethany again had only made her more certain than ever that Ma was mistaken. Now she had to find a way to prove that to Ma, because she couldn't bear to lose Bethany as a friend.

"I'd better go," she said reluctantly. "It's getting late."

"I'll walk a ways with you," Bethany said.

Esther thanked Mrs. Klause for lunch. Then she set out for home with Bethany at her side. Esther carried one of the buckets of berries. Bethany carried the other. They sang songs as they walked, and they played follow the leader. They took turns deciding whether to strut or walk sideways or backward—whether to carry the buckets in their right hand or their left or even on top of their heads. Bethany walked a long way with Esther, but finally she had to turn and go back home.

She handed her bucket to Esther. With a sad smile she said, "I wish you could come every day." Then she waved. "See you at church."

Esther smiled and waved, too, but her heart slid down toward her stomach as she remembered Ma. Was it possible for her to stay friends with Bethany without Ma knowing? She always seemed to know everything. Esther chewed her lip and trudged down the roadside, thinking hard. Sunday school was held away from the parents. That was not the problem. It was before and after that was the trouble. Of course, a lot of people milled around before and after services. Esther might be able to say quick hellos and good-byes to Bethany without Ma noticing. She would just have to be very careful.

Suddenly she thought of Violet. There would be no way to hide the friendship from her. And her older sister might feel it was her duty to tell Ma that Esther was still seeing Bethany. But Esther did not think so. Violet didn't take signs as seriously as Ma did. Esther believed Violet's sympathy would keep her silent.

Esther was not happy with her plan. She didn't like the idea of sneaking behind Ma's back. But the thought of hurting Bethany somehow seemed even worse.

When Esther returned home, Ma praised her for picking so many berries. Esther could barely meet her mother's eyes. Ma could read so many signs. Could she see on Esther's face that she had deceived her? Esther's cheeks burned at the thought. But all Ma said was, "Next time remember to wear a hat. Your face is red from the sun." She even rested her cool, rough hand against Esther's cheek for a moment.

Esther nodded because she could not speak. She was too ashamed. How could she go on lying to Ma? But if she didn't, how could she tell Bethany that Ma said she was marked? Esther didn't know if she would ever be able to decide which was worse. If only Julia would hurry and answer her letter. Esther needed some good advice.

Surprisingly, there was word from Julia that very night, but not what anyone expected. The family had just finished supper when they heard Mickey barking. A few moments later a car door slammed. They all looked at one another in surprise. Who could it be? Pa rose and went to the screen door. Mr. Brummel appeared on the porch. A big man with shaggy white hair and a shy smile, he always made Esther think of a sheepdog.

"Good news," he announced to a chorus of fairy bells as Pa invited him inside. "I bring you good news." Because Mr. Brummel was the sheriff, he had one of the few telephones in the area. Important messages were often relayed through him. He pumped Pa's hand and clapped him on the back. "Your daughter Julia just telephoned. She asked me to tell you that her sister had her baby tonight. A boy! Henry Christian. Both he and his mama are fine."

Pa beamed at Ma. She smiled and urged Mr. Brummel to sit. "You must have a bowl of raspberries and cream," she invited. She scurried across the kitchen for another bowl. "One month early but the baby is fine. And he is named after his grandpa! We have much to celebrate."

"I'm an aunt!" Violet suddenly cried.

"Me too!" Esther said. She turned to Walter. "And you're an uncle."

He laughed. "I'm not an uncle. I'm a boy."

But she explained, and she knew he finally understood when his mouth fell open. "I'm Uncle Walter," he crowed, and everyone laughed.

That night, Esther lay awake in bed for a long time. It had been such a special day, she wanted to press the happy memories firmly into her mind so she'd never forget.

If only she could shake off the sad feeling that came whenever she thought about disobeying Ma. Esther had always tried hard to please Ma and to be good, but here she was doing something Ma had strictly forbidden! She had barely been able to eat her raspberries after supper. Each one was like a pebble of guilt added to the heavy pile already inside her.

"*Nu*, Esther, are you not well?" Ma had asked. "Did so much sun make you sick?" She had frowned in worry.

"No, Ma, I'm fine," Esther had told her. "I ate a lot of berries while I was picking, though." That much at least was true. If only everything could be true. If only life today could be as simple as it had been a week ago, when Esther had no secrets.

The last thing she heard before she drifted off to sleep was a gentle drumming on the roof. It took Esther a few moments to realize what it was. Then she smiled. It was raining at last.

9 Harvest Time

AUGUST MARKED THE BEGINNING OF THE harvest. There was no time to write long grumbly letters. There was no time for picnics. There was little time even to play with Mickey and Margaret.

Suppers were late so they could all work longer. Pa usually fell asleep in his rocker reading the day-old copy of the *Wisconsin State Journal* he got for free at the dairy. Walter sometimes fell asleep right at the table. And Esther and Violet were yawning long before they finished washing the dishes. Ma, her knitting needles clicking, was always the last one to bed. She was making mittens and scarves and wool stockings. Just looking at them made Esther feel hotter than ever. Winter seemed very far away.

Esther and Violet spent much of each day working in Ma's vegetable garden. The crops in the fields had suffered from the lack of rain. But thanks to the well, the garden had thrived.

All summer Ma had carried heavy buckets of water from the well to soak the dry ground. Now tomatoes, cabbages, beets, carrots, onions, cucumbers, beans, and green peppers were all ripening at once. Every day the girls picked the ripest ones and carried them indoors. Ma boiled them in big pots of water and stored them in glass jars. She pickled the cucumbers and some of the beets and onions and stored those in glass jars, too. It was hot, hot work, but it meant they would have vegetables even in the winter.

When the vegetable garden began to slow down, the grapes in the arbor were ripe. And the plum trees were heavy with fruit. The girls picked fruit until their arms ached. Ma filled jar after jar with jams and jellies. And one day, for a treat, she made fry cakes.

Esther loved fry cakes. It was fun to watch Ma drop big spoonfuls of the dough into bubbling hot oil and to watch the dough puff up into airy cakes. When they were golden brown, Ma rolled them in sugar. Just before they were to be eaten, she sliced them and filled them with jelly. Yum! Esther ate so many, Ma said she'd be sick, and she was a little. But it was worth it.

Meanwhile, the threshers Pa hired came to harvest

the oats and the wheat with their big machine. Pa was disappointed. There were not nearly so many bushels as he'd hoped. It had been too dry. His hopes were all pinned on the corn and potato crops now. Nothing must go wrong with them.

School started again right after Labor Day. Now Esther could see Bethany every day without looking over her shoulder, watching for Ma. But happy as Esther was to be back in school again, and to have so much more time with Bethany, her guilt at deceiving Ma was always with her. Like her own little cloud, it cast a small shadow over even her brightest days.

Sometimes Esther would be playing with Bethany and she'd suddenly imagine Ma had come up behind her. She'd see the shock on Ma's face that Esther had disobeyed her, and she would vow to tell Bethany the truth. But when she looked into Bethany's smiling face, the words stuck in her throat. She could not tell her friend that Ma thought she was marked and dangerous. She could not.

Sometimes it made Esther angry that she felt guilty all the time. Angry with Ma for thinking Bethany's mole was a sign. Angry with Pa for not telling Ma she was wrong this time. Even angry with Bethany—for being too nice to hurt, and for having that darned old mole to begin with. But mostly Esther was angry with herself, because she couldn't find a way out of the lie that would not hurt someone.

That year, Walter was in first grade and Miss Larson was his teacher. But Esther and Bethany had moved up to fifth grade, so they were in Violet's room. Their teacher was Mrs. Davies.

"She's not as young and pretty as Miss Larson," Esther had observed to Bethany on the first day of school. "But she's awfully nice. I think I'll like her all right, don't you?"

Bethany nodded. "She puts on a play every year, too. Now we'll be able to be in it with the rest of the big kids."

Esther's heart gave a little hop. A play! She'd always wanted to be in a play. "When is it?" she asked eagerly.

"The play's not until spring, but we'll start working on it right after the New Year. Hannah Peterson told me it was the most fun she ever had," Bethany reported. "They make all the scenery and everything!"

Esther didn't need any convincing. She was sure being in a play would be the most wonderful thing ever. If only winter weren't so far away!

September slipped past in a warm, green haze. October arrived dressed in vivid oranges, reds, and golds. Esther couldn't remember ever seeing leaves as bright as the ones she saw that fall. Every morning she stood for a few moments on the porch to look at the maples and elms that skirted the house. And every morning they were more beautiful. The maples turned fiery red. The elms turned bronze and gold—so gold, they seemed to glow.

"It's almost like magic," Esther whispered to Mickey. "I half expect to see fairies dancing on the branches."

One morning when Esther and Violet arrived in their classroom, all the children were talking about the Nielson twins. Neither boy was present, but their cousin, an eighth-grade girl named Katrina, announced that they were moving.

"Uncle's crops were poor again this year," she explained. "He can't pay what he owes, so the bank is auctioning off their farm on Saturday."

"But what will happen to Wes and Thomas?" Esther asked.

Katrina shrugged. "I don't know. Uncle is talking about moving to Madison or Milwaukee. But farming is the only work he knows."

The news weighed on Esther's heart for the rest of the day. Listening to Walter's class say the letters of the alphabet lifted her spirits some. But when she came back to her classroom and saw the twins' empty desks, her sadness returned.

That night, before he got up from the table after supper, Pa told Ma about the auction. "Brummel told me when I ran into him at the dairy this morning," he said. "It is sad, sad news."

"I'm glad that could never happen to us," Esther said. "We'll live here forever!"

Pa's forehead wrinkled. "We have a mortgage, too, *Liebling*," he said gently. "Another summer like this one and who knows? The auction could be here."

"But I thought we owned the farm," she protested.

"Not completely," Pa explained. "We used our savings to pay for part of it. But the rest is a loan from the bank—that's the mortgage. If the mortgage is not paid back, the bank takes back the land and sells it to someone else."

Esther slumped in her chair. First there was the rain to worry about, and now this. Wasn't life ever certain? Wasn't anything forever?

When the dishes were washed, Pa brought out the checkerboard. Violet and Walter scooted over to grab chairs. With most of the crops harvested, Pa's labors had eased a little. More and more often he played checkers or rummy in the evening. But that night Esther was not in a mood for games.

She went out and sat on the porch steps. Mickey padded over. He lay down beside her and rested his head in her lap. She stroked his velvety ears and looked out at the farm. The sun was just setting over the harvested wheat field. Esther's heart swelled at the purple and gold beauty of it.

She had never really noticed sunsets in Chicago. She had never eaten berries she'd picked herself. She'd never eaten vegetables she'd helped to grow. She'd never sat on her very own porch with her very own dog. She had never felt such a tie to anyplace as she felt to the farm.

"I don't ever want to leave, Mickey." She gulped. "Not ever. Not even if we never get a bathroom in the house."

Mickey's tail thumped against the floorboards. She knew that meant he understood. It meant he didn't ever want her to leave, either.

All that week Esther thought hard. She wanted to find a way to help pay the mortgage. Then they could stay on the farm forever. And then Ma would see that she could do something important for the family. Surely she would be impressed by that. But what could Esther do? In *Little Women*, Jo had sold her hair to help her family. But Esther's hair was not long enough to sell. And she wouldn't know where to take it if it was. Still, there had to be something she could do.

On Friday after school, Esther got an idea. The hazelnut and walnut trees behind the farmhouse were full of nuts. She'd gather the ones that had fallen on the ground and sell them at the roadside on Saturday. Excited, she rummaged in the barn until she found an old wooden crate.

"Can I use this, Pa?"

Pa looked up from the harness he was cleaning. He nodded. "What will you use it for?"

Esther smiled. "It's a surprise. Do you have any paint?"

"Just a few drops of black." He gestured to a small can on the shelf.

He was right. There wasn't much. But Esther didn't need much. She swirled a brush around the inside of the can to get every last bit of paint. She was just able to write *NUTS 5c* before it ran out. Then she took two empty feed sacks and ran out back. Nuts were thick on the four trees. But they were thick on the ground, too, and much handier. Squirrels ran away and scolded when Esther scooped up the nuts and dropped them into a sack.

"You can climb the trees," she scolded back. "Don't be so lazy."

It was suppertime before she quit and dragged both sacks to the back porch. Ma had just come outside to call her. She blinked at Esther and the sacks in surprise. "*Nu,* what have you been up to?"

"I've been gathering nuts," Esther told her proudly. "I'm going to sell them along the road tomorrow. The money will help pay the mortgage."

She held her breath and waited for Ma's reaction. Would she laugh? Would she shake her head and say it was a waste of time? Or would she tell Esther she was a genius, and that she loved her with all her heart?

Ma did neither of those things. She nodded and said, "A good idea." Then she smiled down at Esther and said it again. "A good idea."

Esther was chilled from being outdoors for so long. But Ma's words warmed her better than any fire, from the inside out. She smiled back at Ma and followed her into the house.

After supper, Ma gave Esther a stack of old newspapers. She showed her how to make cones from the paper. The cones could be filled with nuts and then twisted shut on top. "Just be sure to mark the walnut bags with a *W* or you will not know which are which," Ma cautioned her. She even gave Esther a stub of pencil for the job.

Esther was overjoyed. Ma was really noticing her! And she was proud of what Esther was trying to do. Esther could see it in her eyes. Just wait until I hand her and Pa a pile of money tomorrow, Esther thought. She'll hug me then for sure, just like Mrs. Rubinstein hugged Shirley.

The next morning, right after breakfast, Esther lugged the crate out to the roadside. It was heavy now that it was stuffed with bags of nuts. Esther thought about asking Violet, or even Walter, to help her carry it. But then they might feel they had some claim to the glory when she handed the money over later. No. It was better to stagger and pant and stumble.

At the roadside Esther emptied the crate, sorting the paper bundles into two piles, ones marked with a *W* and ones that were not. Then she turned the crate on end so drivers could read the sign she'd painted. There would be lots of cars and wagons passing soon. On Saturdays many families went to town for supplies. Her nuts would make a tempting treat to buy along the way. Esther patted her lucky birthday hair ribbon and perched on the bottom rail of the fence to wait.

Sure enough, it wasn't long before cars began to rumble past. But they weren't the farmers Esther was expecting. They were men in suits and ties driving big, shiny cars. They drove by with hardly a glance at Esther's sign.

The sun climbed higher. Esther paced back and forth and squinted down the road. Where were her customers? Soon she would have to go home for lunch, and she hadn't sold even one bag. What would Ma say? She would think Esther 's idea had been a foolish one after all.

Suddenly Esther heard a car coming from the direction of town. When it came nearer, she saw it was one of the shiny cars she'd seen earlier. It lurched to a stop, sending up a spray of dirt and gravel. The driver called, "What have you got?"

"Hazels and walnuts," Esther called back.

"I'll take two of each," he said.

Thrilled, Esther brought him the nuts. But when the man handed her a quarter, her heart sank. "I don't have any change," she told him. Would he give the nuts back and drive away?

He waved his hand. "You can have the nickel," he said. Then he roared away.

Almost immediately another car came. This car had three men in it. Between them they bought eight bags of nuts!

"At least I'll have made one good buy today," one of the men grumbled. The others snorted and laughed.

Three more cars of strangers passed by. Esther watched hopefully, but they didn't slow. One red-faced driver was waving his fist and talking to his passengers. Esther wondered how he managed to stay on the road.

After a while, the farm wagons and cars she'd expected finally began to come. But not headed *toward* town—coming *from* town. And instead of families, most of them carried men and older boys. Many of them stopped and bought nuts from Esther. They were all in high spirits and laughing heartily.

"Did you see the look on his face when we gave it to him?" one man said, slapping his knee. "By Jove, that was a look I'll never forget."

The other men—men Esther recognized by face if not by name—were loud in their agreement. What was going on? But she had no time to puzzle it out. She had to scamper to fill orders. Then a car stopped and Pa jumped out. By this time, Esther's curiosity was past controlling.

"What's going on, Pa? Where've you all been?"

Pa swooped Esther up and twirled her around. His

whole face was a smile. "We did something good today, *Liebling*. We saved the Nielson farm."

Esther gasped. "How?"

Pa set her down on the crate. "All the farmers from twenty miles around went to the auction. We got there very early. Before anyone else. We blocked all the roads leading to the farm so no one else could get through. When the auctioneer asked for bids, the only one he got was from us—five dollars!" Pa laughed. "Such a look he got on his face! But he had to take it. And then we gave the farm back to Nielson. So he will not be moving after all."

Esther jumped up and down, clapping her hands. "You're heroes!"

Pa shook his head. "Not heroes, Esther. Just good neighbors."

Esther felt very proud later when she handed Ma and Pa the cigar box of coins she'd earned. One dollar and fifty-five cents in all! The look on Pa's face was worth all her work and more. But Ma, what would Ma do? Esther trembled with anticipation.

Ma slowly reached out and touched Esther's cheek. Her hands were red and work worn, but her touch was soft. Esther felt as if her heart might fly right out of her body it was beating so fast. *"Nu,"* said Ma. "You did good work, Esther. Very good work."

It had not been a hug, but it had been so nearly one

that Esther was satisfied. Ma was proud of her. The hug that would prove she *loved* her was coming closer all the time.

For the rest of the day Esther thought about how Pa had helped to save the Nielsons' farm. He and the other men had come up with a daring plan. And it had worked. Now Wes and Thomas wouldn't have to move away.

"He is a hero," she whispered to Margaret that night. "No matter what Pa says, he's a hero." It had been a while since Esther had thought of Rin Tin Tin. But she thought of him now. She remembered thinking that Rin Tin Tin was a hero. But Rin Tin Tin only saved people from pretend disasters. Pa had saved people from a real one.

10 The Halloween Party

"I'LL NEVER BE ABLE TO MAKE A COSTUME out of these things," Esther complained. She turned the flame of the kerosene lamp higher and surveyed the odds and ends on the table. There was an old, old shirt of Pa's, much tattered and torn. There was a pair of his overalls. There were two mismatched work gloves, each lacking a couple of fingertips. And there was a battered and stained straw hat. Esther groaned in despair. "A witch's cape would be *so* much easier."

Violet looked up from her arithmetic homework. She glanced over her shoulder into the parlor. "Don't let Ma hear you," she warned in a whisper. "You know what she said about you dressing like a witch."

Esther sighed. Ma had been furious that Esther

would even suggest such a thing. "You make fun of things you do not understand," she had scolded. "That can be dangerous."

There was that word again. *Dangerous.* First Bethany and now witch costumes were dangerous. But Esther had seen lots of children dress as witches in Chicago. Nothing bad had happened to them.

"Look at this shirt," she grumbled. "It's got about a hundred holes in it! And the overalls are way too big. But I can't cut them 'cause Pa needs them back."

"Scarecrows are supposed to be goofy looking," Violet tried to comfort her.

But Esther only got more upset. "I don't want to look goofy. I want to look scary!" She jumped to her feet, bared her teeth, and waved claw-like hands in the air.

"R-r-r-r-r!"

On the porch, Mickey was startled into barking. Even Esther had to let go of her bad temper to laugh. She had frightened Mickey even without a costume. She supposed she really was making too much of things.

She probably didn't have a chance of winning the silver-dollar prize no matter what. Sarah Sanderson's mother was making her a princess costume with real sequins on the sleeves. Nothing would beat that. Still, it would have been nice to hand that silver dollar to Ma after the party. "More money toward the mortgage," she would say. And wouldn't Ma be proud of her then!

Oh well, Esther thought. Maybe next year. She was going to the church Halloween party. That was the important thing. The party was less than a week away, so there was no time to waste.

If only Julia were there. Julia was a real seamstress, like Ma. She could do anything with a needle and thread. She would turn the pile of old clothes into a splendid costume, easy as pie. Even Violet might have been a help. But she was too busy with homework and her own costume.

So Esther was on her own, and she was all thumbs with a needle. She had to start somewhere, though. She frowned and set the gloves aside. They could be worn as they were. And, awful as the hat was, it, too, would do. After all, as Violet had pointed out, scarecrows weren't supposed to be stylish. That left her with the shirt and overalls. She looked from one to the other. Well, at least she knew what she had to do with the shirt. She set her jaw, laid the pants aside, and started stitching torn seams.

At school, everyone was talking about the coming party.

"They served ice cream last year," Thomas reminded everyone daily.

"And caramel apples," someone else would add.

"And popcorn balls," another voice would chime in.

Esther's mouth watered just thinking about such treats.

"This week is going by so slow!" Bethany complained on Wednesday. "I feel like Friday's never going to come."

"I just hope I can finish my costume in time," Esther said. "The shirt's finally done, but I still don't know what to do about the overalls. Even with the legs rolled up and the straps as high as they'll go, they're way too long."

"Why don't you ask your mother for help? Likely she'll have an idea," Bethany suggested.

Esther didn't want to admit she was still sulking because Ma wouldn't let her be a witch. She just said, "We'll see."

The next day, after school, she found a fat letter from Julia in the mailbox. Quickly Esther ripped open the envelope as Walter raced ahead to the house. Then, walking slowly, she read the letter aloud to Violet.

October 20, 1930

Dear Esther,

I loved your story about how the farmers saved your neighbors' land. I wish people in the city cared as much about one another. More and more families are being evicted from their homes because they've lost their jobs and can't pay the rent. Now that Howard's workdays have been cut, he and Kate are gladder than ever that I'm with them. The money I give them toward the rent and food is a real help.

Little Henry is thriving. Yes, he smiles quite a lot. He's a good baby and Kate is a wonderful mother. She can't wait to show him off when we visit you at Thanksgiving.

Good news! David found a job at last. It's hard work. He unloads trucks all day. But he's so glad to be earning money again, he doesn't mind his sore muscles.

Now for the real reason for this letter. I haven't forgotten that you asked for my advice about Bethany and Ma. I just wanted to understand some things better before I tried to explain them to you. So last week I visited Aunt Olga. She told me more about Ma's life in Russia.

You know that when Ma was eleven, her mother died. Because she was the oldest girl, Ma had to cook and clean while her father and older brother worked in the fields. And she had to take care of her little brothers and sisters. One of them was a little sister named Tatiana.

"Tatiana!" Violet exclaimed. "Isn't she the sister Aunt Olga said looked so much like you?"

Esther nodded impatiently. "Yes. But hush while I finish the letter."

Ma loved all her brothers and sisters, but Tatiana was especially dear to her. Ma couldn't resist her smiles and playfulness. Instead of insisting that Tatiana obey, Ma often gave in to her, and she gave her lots of attention. One day—although she'd been told many times to stay away from it—Tatiana went wading in their stream, and she drowned. Ma was brokenhearted. She said she had *angered the fairies by ignoring them and spoiling Tatiana. She insisted that what happened to Tatiana was her fault, her punishment. Aunt Olga says Ma was never the same after that. To protect the other children, she became more and more superstitious.*

Esther had to stop reading. Her eyes were filled with tears. "Poor Ma," she gulped. "She told me about Tatiana's accident, but she didn't tell me that she blamed herself for it."

Violet sniffled. "And Ma was so young."

Esther wiped her eyes with the back of her hand and lifted the letter again.

I'm sorry, Esther. I know none of this tells you how to change what Ma believes about Bethany. I don't know if there is a way to do that. But I'm hoping this story will help you to understand why superstitions have such a hold on Ma.

My goodness, this letter has gotten long! I have to stop or I'll be late for work.

Be sure to write and tell me all about the party.

Happy Halloween!

> *Heaps of Love,*
> *Julia*

Esther folded the letter carefully. Automatically she put it back in its envelope and tucked it into her reader. She was deep in thought. No wonder Ma believed in superstitions and signs. She had seen them come horribly true. Maybe all the wishing in the world could not change her.

That night, Esther swallowed her pride and asked Ma for help with her costume. Ma took one look at Esther in Pa's overalls and shook with laughter. But a moment later she darted out of the room. When she came back, she had Pa's belt in her hand. "Pull the pants up at your waist," she instructed.

Esther pulled them up. Ma put the belt around Esther's middle and buckled it snugly. Next, she rolled up the bottoms of the long legs. Finally, she crisscrossed the straps three times in the back before pulling them over Esther's shoulders to fasten. "There," she said. "Now put on the shirt and the hat and gloves. Let me see what kind of scarecrow you will make."

Esther hurried into the pantry and pulled her dress over her head. Then she slipped her arms into the long sleeves of Pa's old, mended shirt. She was eager to show Ma what she looked like before Ma got involved with something else and forgot her interest in Esther and her costume.

Quickly, Esther buttoned the shirt and slapped the hat onto her head. She was stuffing the shirt into the overalls when she realized the shirt was buttoned crooked. Darn! Ma would notice that for sure and she would scold. Uneven buttoning was bad luck and the only thing to do about it was to unbutton the shirt, take it off, and shake all the bad luck out of it. Then and only then was it safe to put it on again and button it properly.

But Esther was in a hurry. With fumbling fingers she quickly unbuttoned the shirt, gave it a couple of flaps with her arms still in the sleeves—surely that was good enough—and speedily redid the buttons. A minute later she burst out of the pantry and ran to find Ma and Pa in the parlor.

"Ach!" Pa cried. "A scarecrow in the house. What will happen next!" But he was laughing.

Ma smiled and nodded. "You look good," she told Esther.

"I couldn't have done it without you," Esther said. "Thank you, Ma!" Impulsively, she threw her arms around Ma's neck. At once she felt Ma stiffen and pull back. Esther dropped her arms as if she'd been stung. She turned away so Ma wouldn't see the tears flooding her eyes.

"It is time for bed," Ma said quickly, blowing out the flame in the parlor lamp. "Do not forget to leave your door open," she added gently. "It gets cold these nights."

Was Ma sorry that she had pulled away from Esther? Was that why her voice was so soft? Had Esther's hug just startled her? And if Esther had taken the shirt off and shaken out the bad luck before she buttoned it back up, would Ma have hugged her back? Now she would never know.

Violet was in their bedroom brushing her hair in front of the mirror. When she saw Esther, she exclaimed, "The overalls fit! How did you manage it?"

"Ma helped me," Esther said. "Look." She tugged up on the top part of the overalls to reveal the belt. "And . . ." She twisted around to show Violet her back. "The criss-crossing shortens the straps a lot." Esther's excitement about the costume contest was quickly returning. Maybe she had a chance at the silver-dollar prize after all.

"Tomorrow night I'll put flour on my face. I'll have straw sticking out of my shirt and gloves and hat. I'll look just like a real scarecrow." She glanced at Violet's colorful costume hanging on the back of the door. "You'll make a pretty gypsy," she said. "But wouldn't you rather be scary?"

Violet shook her head. "Nope. I'd rather be beautiful and mysterious." She fluttered her eyelashes. They had finally grown back. Violet was convinced they were longer and thicker than before. Esther was just as sure they were not, but she knew better than to say so. She twirled around happily.

"I can't wait 'til tomorrow!" she sang.

The next day at school seemed to last forever. Even recess was too long. But finally Mrs. Davies rang the bell. School was dismissed.

"Be sure to come early," Bethany reminded Esther as they bounded down the school steps. "We don't want to miss any of the fun."

"I'll be there as early as I can," Esther promised. Walter was tossing his cap in the air. "Walter, put your hat on your head before it lands in a mud puddle," she scolded. Then she waved one last time to her friend. "Bye, Bethany. See you at the party!"

Violet joined Esther and Walter and they started for home. Their steps were lighter and faster than usual. It wasn't long before they arrived at the old farmhouse. Ma had just finished making Walter's pirate costume. He was so excited, he had to try on the black vest and eye patch at once.

"You're perfect!" Esther said when he strutted around the kitchen, waving his cardboard sword.

"Can we go to the party now?" Walter asked Ma.

"No, not now. The party is not until after supper," she explained.

"But can we go early?" Walter persisted. "Bethany told Esther to be sure an' go early so we don't miss any of the fun."

Esther's heart stopped.

Ma stiffened. Then, slowly, slowly she turned to level a piercing look at Esther. "Bethany?" Ma repeated. "Why would Bethany say this to you when you are not friends with her anymore?"

Esther's heart exploded into a wild pounding. Her face was on fire. Her mouth was suddenly so dry, her tongue seemed stuck. How could she explain? Ma would never understand. Never! Esther could barely meet Ma's stern gaze. Her knees began to shake. "I-I—" she tried to speak.

But Walter was faster. "Esther and Bethany are so friends," he told Ma. "Best friends, like me an' Lars. Right, Esther?" He turned to grin at her, but seeing Esther's face, his grin wobbled uncertainly.

"Walter, go to your room," Ma said quietly. He fled. "Violet, go peel potatoes for supper." Violet threw Esther a look of sympathy and vanished into the kitchen. For a long moment Ma just looked at Esther. She was angry. But there was something in her face besides anger. Something Esther had never seen there before. Disappointment, yes. But also pain. Esther had *hurt* Ma. Esther bit her lip, trying not to cry. Ma hated tears.

At last, when Esther could not bear the quiet another second, Ma spoke. "You have disobeyed me," she said. She said it so sadly that Esther couldn't help it. She did cry then.

"I'm sorry, Ma," she sobbed. "I didn't want to. I just couldn't do what you wanted. I tried, but I couldn't. She's my friend. She's been my friend for all these months and nothing bad has happened. Don't you think you could be wrong just this once?" Esther pleaded.

"*Nu!*" Ma exclaimed. "How can you say nothing bad

has happened? You disobey me. You become a sneaky child I cannot trust. Are these not bad things?" Ma shook her head as if it were suddenly too heavy for her shoulders. "When I tell you something, it is for your own good. You are not to question."

Esther hung her head, too miserable to speak.

Ma sighed. "You must be punished," she said more quietly. "So you will remember to obey the next time. Look at me."

Esther looked at Ma. She saw disappointment and sadness on Ma's face that she hoped never to see there again. "You will not go to the party tonight," Ma said. Esther heard a gasp from the kitchen. "And from now on, you will stay away from Bethany. Do you understand?"

Esther nodded blindly. Tears spilled down her cheeks and splashed onto her dress.

That night, the family drove off to the party without her. Esther ran to her room, clutched Margaret to her heart, and threw herself onto her bed. She cried so hard that Mickey howled in distress on the porch. She cried because she was missing the party. She cried because she could never be friends with Bethany again. But most of all, she cried because she had disappointed Ma so terribly. Maybe she would never love Esther now.

11 Thanksgiving

November 8, 1930

Dear Julia,

I did it. I told Bethany we cannot be friends anymore. I did not tell her why. I could not tell her Ma says she is marked and dangerous! I just said that Ma had forbidden it. Bethany looked so sad. She ran into the outhouse. And when she came out, her eyes were all red. I felt awful. I still do. Now I spend recess reading at my desk while Bethany and the other girls play outside. It is very lonely. The only thing that cheers me up is thinking about you and Kate and Howard and little Henry coming for Thanksgiving. Mickey and I will show you all around the farm. I just hope it is nicer weather than it is today.

Esther raised her head and watched raindrops dribble down the kitchen window. She'd planned to ride Bruno around the pasture today. She was going to pretend they were leading a circus parade. Then the rain had come.

Even Esther's walk to the mailbox had ended badly, since she'd been so excited to find a letter from Julia that she ran into the kitchen without wiping her feet. Ma, who had just finished mopping the floor, started to scold about muddy footprints. Then she spotted the open umbrella Esther still held in her hand.

"Nu!" She shook her finger at Esther. "Close that umbrella right now! You know you call bad luck into our house when you bring an open umbrella inside."

"I'm sorry, Ma!" Esther cried, dropping the letter on the table and struggling to snap the umbrella shut. Ma took it from Esther and marched over to the door. She put the umbrella on the back porch and then, for the second time that morning, scrubbed furiously at the patch of floor in front of it.

Esther slunk away to her bedroom to read Julia's letter about baby Henry, her job at the telephone company, and how they were all counting the days until Thanksgiving. But it was too chilly to stay up in her room for long, so now Esther was downstairs again, hoping against hope that the rain would stop before the entire day was wasted.

She watched Walter shoot a marble across the parlor floor, trying to get it inside a circle of string. She looked across the table at Violet sketching dresses on the backs of old envelopes. Everyone had something fun to do but her. If only there were a library in town. In Chicago, Esther always had books to read. A rainy day like this one was perfect for reading. Esther sighed. A moment later, her stomach rumbled.

"Can I have a slice of bread, Ma?" she asked. "I'm hungry."

Ma was cutting off the tops of green peppers at the sink. She looked at Esther. "It will not be long until supper. Try to wait."

Esther sighed again. Then she asked hopefully, "Are you making porcupines?"

"Almost porcupines," Ma replied, lining the peppers upright in a pan.

"Almost?" Esther repeated. "How can they be 'almost porcupines'?"

"They will have no meat inside, just rice and tomato," Ma explained.

"Oh." Esther didn't have to ask why. She already knew the answer. Money. The corn had indeed grown well, but prices had been low. The potatoes had done well, too, but some had to be kept for the family. And some were special seed potatoes to be planted in the spring. There were not as many potatoes left to sell as Pa would have liked.

Pa looked up from the paper he'd been figuring on. "We made just enough to pay the bills, nothing extra."

His voice sounded tired. "Maybe I did wrong to bring us here." The creases in Pa's face looked deeper than usual.

"It is just one harvest," Ma said. "We will find ways to manage. You will see. Next year will be better. It was not wrong to come here."

Pa had already sold Blossom, the new calf he had hoped to keep. And he had sold all but two of the grown-up piglets. He traded one of the remaining two pigs to Mr. Brummel for bushels of barley. The other pig had been turned into ham and bacon for the family.

"I will have to sell the sow," he said, dropping his pencil onto the table. "And then there will be no pigs to sell next fall."

"With good crops we will not need the extra money," Ma said.

Pa bobbled his head twice, but his mouth was still turned down at the corners. "Three of the cows are going dry now, too. We will lose most of the milk money for a while."

"You are worrying about spring. Worry about something much nearer," Ma suggested. "Thanksgiving. It will be our family's first time together in months. It must be perfect. But how, when we have so little?"

"We could go to the church dinner," Esther suggested. "Then we'd just have to bring a few pies or a big bowl of potatoes."

Ma shook her head. "We could do that if it were just us. But to bring another whole family of outsiders, no. It would not be right."

Pa smiled at Ma. "You will manage, Anna. You always do."

And somehow Ma did. Over the weeks that followed, she traded with their neighbors to get the foods she did not have. Jars of plum jam were traded for yams. Walnuts and jars of raspberry preserves were exchanged for apples and pumpkins. And instead of a turkey, she decided—much to Esther's delight—they would roast one of the geese.

But the night before a goose was to be sacrificed, Mr. Brummel brought another message from Julia. This time he was not smiling. The baby was sick with diphtheria. They could not think of coming. They would call again when they knew more.

"Oh, no," Ma said, sinking onto the nearest chair and covering her mouth with her hands.

Esther felt cold all over. Diphtheria! People *died* of diphtheria.

The holiday was forgotten. All anyone could think of was the tiny baby none of them had even seen yet. He was so little. Would he be strong enough to fight off such a terrible illness?

That night before they went to bed, they all gathered in the parlor. Ma took the precious iron cross from the fireplace mantel and held it while Pa said a prayer asking for Henry Christian's recovery. Esther had never prayed so hard before. But would their prayers be enough to save the baby? Could the iron cross's protection stretch all the way to Chicago?

The next day, for the first time ever, Esther did not want to go to school. She wanted to be home when the next message came, and so did Violet and Walter. Ma and Pa understood and allowed them to stay home with them.

That was the longest day Esther could remember. The house was quiet, like it was holding its breath. There was no laughter, no chatter, just dragging footsteps and worried faces. Even Walter went about with serious eyes and a hushed voice.

Thanksgiving morning arrived, and still there was no word. But Pa was determined to be cheerful. "The baby will be all right," he said at breakfast. "I have faith all will be well. You must all have faith, too."

Ma sighed softly but nodded. Esther nodded, too. Pa was right. It was Thanksgiving Day—a day to count blessings. The baby was one of their blessings. They had to believe he would not be taken from them.

Ma began to clear the table. "I never made the pies," she said suddenly.

Pa laughed. "And I never butchered the goose. I suppose we could just have one of the chickens now, since it will only be the five of us." He directed a questioning look at Ma.

She puckered her mouth as she considered. "Maybe we should go to the church dinner after all," she said slowly.

Pa was quick to nod. "That is a good idea. We will be with our neighbors."

Esther looked at Violet and Walter. She saw them sit up straighter in anticipation. Suddenly it felt like a holiday.

Even though it was morning and the middle of the week, Ma brought in the tub. Quickly, quickly everyone bathed and dressed. Quickly, quickly Ma boiled and beat potatoes until they were light and fluffy. She cooked carrots and topped them with the last of the fresh butter she had been saving. Then she wrapped everything well in thick layers of old newspaper to keep it hot.

Pa carried the food out to the buggy. "Time to go," he said.

Esther was waiting her turn to get into the buggy when she noticed something odd. "Ma," she said, pointing at the sky. "It's the moon! And it's daytime. How can that be?"

Ma gazed up at the white circle in the bright blue sky. She frowned.

"What does it mean, Anna?" Pa asked anxiously.

"It means a change is coming," she said.

"A good one or a bad one?" Violet asked.

Ma shook her head. "Just a change." She looked at Pa. "It could be good or bad."

Pa stood silent for a moment. Then he nodded. "Come," he said, swinging Walter up into the front seat. "We don't want to be late."

On the way to town, Esther tried not to think about the change that was coming. A sign that could mean a good or a bad thing seemed worse than no sign at all. You didn't know how to feel or what to think.

A change for little Henry could mean healing or . . . Esther would not let herself even think of what else it could mean. Instead, she looked at the empty fields. She remembered Pa walking through them last July before the rains finally came, clouds of dust rising from his footsteps. She remembered the long, hot days when the threshers had come. She remembered how she and Violet had carried in bushel after bushel of vegetables from the garden—food that Ma had planted and watered so all of them could eat through the winter.

Suddenly Esther understood how the pilgrims must have felt so long ago. Planting crops and harvesting them in a new land—that was what her family had done. Now the crops were safely gathered and, moon or no, it was time to give thanks.

Esther hardly recognized the church basement where Sunday school was always held. Today it was crammed with tables and people. At one end was the long serving table. On it there were four enormous turkeys. There were bowls and bowls of potatoes, vegetables, and stuffing. There were all kinds of rolls and breads. And best of all, there were pies of every description.

The babble of voices suddenly hushed. Reverend Phillips went to stand behind the serving table to say grace. He thanked God for a bountiful harvest and for friends, families, and health. Then he added, "And dear Father in heaven, we ask that you please watch over and heal the Vogels' new grandson, Henry Christian. Amen."

Ma and Pa looked surprised but very, very pleased. "Brummel must have told the Reverend," Pa said. "I will be sure to thank him. So many people's prayers added to ours!" He cleared his throat and shook his head. Then, with a quick wipe at his eyes, he gave a little laugh and said, "Enough. Let us eat."

Esther followed Ma and Pa to the end of the food line. When it was their turn, Ma had to help Walter. But Esther and Violet could help themselves. Esther's mouth watered as she filled her plate with turkey, stuffing, vegetables, potatoes, gravy, and corn bread. Last of all she chose a big slice of apple pie. Then she followed Ma and Pa to one of the tables.

They were not really tables. They were long boards laid on top of sawhorses. Three or four families could fit around just one of them, they were so big. Ma and Pa went to the table where the Nielsons and Heggersmiths were sitting.

As she took her seat, Esther noticed Bethany and her family at the next table over. Automatically her heart gave a joyful leap that was followed at once by a sad thud. She had to stop thinking of Bethany as her friend. Esther was about to look away when Bethany glanced up and spotted her. Her dimples flashed in a grin that disappeared an instant later. It seemed that Bethany was having the same problem as Esther.

Esther sadly turned away. She spread her napkin on her lap. But then she couldn't help it. She stole another look at her old friend. Her eyes ran smack into Bethany's all over again. Esther flinched and looked away guiltily.

"So much good food," Ma said to Mrs. Nielson.

"Yes. It truly is a Thanksgiving feast," Mrs. Nielson agreed.

Wesley waggled his eyebrows at Esther and she grinned. She put a forkful of turkey into her mouth. Mmmm. It was delicious. She swallowed it quickly and took another, bigger forkful. Then she noticed Wesley stealthily spearing cherries from Thomas's pie and adding them to his own dessert plate. She giggled—and something horrible happened.

The turkey caught in Esther's throat. Suddenly she couldn't breathe. She opened her mouth and tried to gulp some air. But nothing happened. She grabbed at her throat. She tried to cough. She couldn't. Strangled choking sounds were all that would come from her throat.

Desperately Esther looked around for help. Didn't anyone see what was happening to her? But Ma and Pa were turned away, talking to the Nielsons. Violet was on the far side of Walter and didn't see her. And Walter had eyes only for his plate. Frantic, Esther shoved back her chair and staggered to her feet, clutching her throat.

She heard a faraway voice scream, "Help! Someone help Esther!" Then sound faded away. Esther's knees crumpled beneath her, and she floated away into velvety blackness . . .

Excited voices shattered the stillness.

"She's breathing!"

"Thank the Lord!"

Esther's eyes flickered open. Dazed, she sucked in a deep, glorious breath of air. Then another. Blurry faces were all around her. She blinked and the nearest face came clear. Pa. He was kneeling beside her, holding tight to her hand. She was back on her chair. But hadn't she fallen? Her thoughts were fuzzy. Pa must have picked her up.

"Are you all right now, *Liebling*?" he asked in a shaky voice.

Esther nodded weakly. "I-I think so."

Ma was next to Pa. She had one hand over her eyes.

Was she crying? No, of course not. Ma did not cry. Not even when she hurt her ankle and her face turned chalk white. She was probably just embarrassed by the fuss Esther had caused. Suddenly Esther was embarrassed, too. Everywhere she looked, people were staring at her. They were crowded all around her. Even Mr. Klause.

She was very glad when someone called, "Turkey's gettin' cold!" and everyone laughed and moved back to their tables. But first they smiled at Esther. They patted her on her back or on her head if they were near enough. Chairs squealed and scraped across the floor as they sat down again. Silverware clinked against dishes as they went back to eating. Conversations hummed.

Mr. Klause was the last one to go. Esther watched in confusion as Pa gave him a hearty handshake before he went back to his table. Then Ma and Pa sat down, too. But their eyes watched Esther. At first she was afraid to eat. Cautiously she sipped some milk. Then she tried a tiny taste of mashed potatoes, a nibble of stuffing. But it all tasted so good that soon she was eating almost as if nothing had happened.

After dinner, the ladies cleared the tables while the men drank coffee. The children gathered in clusters around the room. The youngest played cave under the serving table, ducking behind its long tablecloth. Esther stared wistfully at Bethany and the rest of her classmates in a knot across the room.

"You should go thank her," Ma said behind her.

Startled, Esther whirled around. "What do you mean? Thank who?"

"The Klause girl," Ma said. "Bethany. She was the first one to see that you were choking. She screamed for someone to help you. And when nothing Pa or I did helped, Bethany said to her father, 'Do like you did when Rose was choking. Save her, Papa!' So he picked you up and turned you upside down. He held you by your ankles and gave you a good shake. The food fell out and you breathed again." Ma shook her head as if she still couldn't quite believe it.

Esther was embarrassed to think Mr. Klause had turned her upside down. Wesley and everyone else must have seen her underwear! Still, she was very grateful to Mr. Klause. He had saved her life. He and Bethany. And now Ma was telling her she should thank Bethany. Could Esther have misunderstood her? She looked the question at Ma.

"I was wrong about the mark," Ma said. "She is a good girl."

Esther's heart pounded. "Does this mean . . . ?"

"Yes." Ma nodded and gave her a little push. "Go, play with your friend."

"Oh! Thank you, Ma!" Esther cried. Then she ran across the room. Bethany's back was to her. Esther tapped her on the shoulder and Bethany spun around. When she saw Esther, she looked surprised, then happy, then surprised all over again.

"Ma sent me," Esther said simply.

Bethany's eyes widened. "Really?"

Esther nodded vigorously. "We can be friends again—if you still want to." Suddenly Esther felt uncertain. After the way she'd had to break off their friendship, maybe Bethany wouldn't want her as a friend again. Maybe—

"If I *want* to!" Bethany shrieked, throwing her arms around Esther. "Of course I want to be friends again. And this time we'll be friends forever."

"Forever," Esther agreed, hugging Bethany back.

That evening, just before they went to bed, Mr. Brummel came by. "Good news! Good news!" he said. "Your daughter called. The baby is much better. They'll write soon, but you are not to worry."

Sometimes Esther forgot to say her prayers, but not that night. "Thank you, God," she prayed as she shivered under the cold covers. "Thank you for the harvest. Thank you for saving me and little Henry. And thank you for letting me be friends with Bethany again. Amen."

12 Christmas

THE WEEKS BEFORE CHRISTMAS WERE strange ones for Esther. At school everyone chattered about the coming holiday and the presents they hoped for. Bethany shared sugar-sprinkled Christmas cookies with her. And Mrs. Davies was reading them a thrilling book called *A Christmas Carol*. But at home there was hardly any mention of the holiday. Ma, when she talked at all, talked about how the hens were laying fewer eggs, and how fast the supplies were going.

"You will need to bring more wood from the wood-pile again," Ma told Pa one cold morning a week into December. She had just carried in the last of the wood stored on the porch.

Pa nodded and set a crock of milk on the table as he

did every morning. "Even Daisy is giving less milk now," he said, blowing on his cold fingers.

"Take that back then and sell it with the rest," Ma said. "If we do without for a few days, we can buy more flour. We are nearly out."

"The children need milk," Pa protested.

"They need bread more," Ma said, and Pa had to agree.

Fewer eggs meant an end to the hard-boiled eggs Esther and Violet and Walter usually took in their lunches. Less flour meant one slice of jam-covered bread instead of two. A few children at school had even less. Most had more. Still, Esther didn't worry. They might have to scrimp, but Ma and Pa would take care of them. It didn't promise to be much of a Christmas, though.

One morning, Esther went out to do her chores and discovered snow had fallen in the night. "Ohhh . . . ," she whispered, staring at the scene before her. White, white, everywhere white. And above everything was a sky of such a brilliant blue it almost hurt to look at it. It was all so beautiful, Esther's throat ached as if she were going to cry.

Then Mickey came running. His coat was covered with snow. When he stopped on the steps in front of Esther, he shook himself and the cold wetness flew at her. She sputtered with laughter.

After breakfast, the children bundled up well and were ready to leave when Ma said, "Wait." Esther saw her look out the frost-edged window toward the barn. "All right. Yes. You can go now."

Esther and Violet were baffled by Ma's odd behavior. They raised their eyebrows at each other as they stepped out onto the porch. Then they stopped. What was that tinkling, jingling sound?

"Santa Claus!" Walter shrieked, hurtling past the girls.

"Pa!" Esther and Violet chorused as Pa came driving up, not in the buggy or the wagon but in a big old-fashioned sleigh. Esther clapped her mittened hands in delight. Then she jumped into the sleigh and snuggled under one of the blankets Pa had put there.

"It is much colder today," Pa said, "so you get to ride."

"I saw this sleigh a hundred times in the corner of the barn," Esther marveled. "But I thought it was a broken wagon because I couldn't see any wheels." She laughed and Violet and Pa joined her. Then she sat back and sighed happily. "I never, ever imagined riding to school in a sleigh." She couldn't wait to tell Julia.

It was the first of many sleigh rides to and from school. But that first ride was the best one, the one Esther would always remember. Such a smooth, free feeling it was to glide over the snow. Not like the bouncy buggy or the bumpy wagon. No, this was like flying. And in the background there was the steady *jring-jring-jring* of the bells on Fritz and Bruno's harness.

On the way home from school each day, Pa stopped

at the mailbox and Esther hopped out to get the mail. There was usually something, if only a few circulars. But one afternoon a few days before Christmas, the box was empty. Esther was disappointed. She'd hoped for a letter from Julia. When she entered the kitchen a few minutes later, though, she saw a little stack of mail on the table.

"How come the mail wasn't in the box?" Esther asked, sorting through the envelopes. Oh, good! There was a letter from Julia after all.

Ma had been knitting. When the door opened, she jumped up and stuffed her knitting into an empty flour sack. "The postman had to deliver something that did not fit in the box," she explained, coming into the kitchen.

"A package?" Esther asked. She and Violet had just been wondering if Julia and Kate would send presents. They couldn't come for Christmas because the weather was too uncertain. They might get caught in a snowstorm. It was the first Christmas the family would not be all together and Esther could hardly even imagine it. She thought presents might help ease her sadness, though.

But Ma shook her head. "Catalogs."

"The new Sears Roebuck catalog?" Violet asked eagerly.

"No, no. Just seed and fertilizer catalogs for Pa," Ma said.

Violet and Esther exchanged looks of disappointment. Meanwhile, Walter took a crumpled paper star from his pocket and tried to smooth it. "Look, Ma," he said. "The Christmas star. It goes on top of the tree. But where is our tree?"

Ma shook her head. "I know nothing about trees. Esther, go into the cellar and get me three potatoes."

"Yes, Ma." Esther tucked her letter into her spelling book. Then she opened the cellar door and climbed down the short ladder. Brrrr! It was cold. Dark, too, except for the light that spilled down from the kitchen. It took Esther's eyes a few moments to adjust and see into the shadowy corners. Ah, there was the potato bin. It was not nearly as full as it had been in October, though.

Esther looked at the bushel baskets of vegetables lined up along the dirt walls. Some were almost empty. None were more than half full. Her eyes skipped to the shelves on the walls. Jars of fruits and vegetables had once crowded those shelves. Now there were many empty spaces. But many months of winter were yet to come. Would there be enough food? Esther felt a chill that had nothing to do with the temperature. Quickly, she chose three potatoes and left the cellar.

"Here, Ma," she said, setting the potatoes in the sink. Then she closed the cellar door and hurried up to her room to read Julia's letter. But it didn't cheer her as she had hoped. Julia's hours at the telephone company had been cut, so she'd be earning less money. Kate had been sick with influenza but was better now.

We all wish there was some way we could be together for the holiday, Julia's letter concluded. *It won't seem like Christmas without you and the rest of the family.*

Esther sighed. It would have been so wonderful to see her sisters again—and to finally meet her little nephew. She pulled her thin sweater tighter and shivered. Even though Pa had cut holes in the floor to let more heat up from the parlor, it was so cold, she could see her breath in the air. She set the letter on Margaret's lap and went downstairs where it was warmer.

On the last day of school before Christmas, Miss Larson and Mrs. Davies gave every one of their students a gingerbread man cookie with raisin eyes. Esther tucked hers safely in her lunch pail so it wouldn't get broken. But Walter was barely settled in the sleigh before he bit off the head of his cookie. Esther tried not to listen to his contented crunching. Violet ate her gingerbread man slowly, rolling her eyes heavenward after each tiny bite. Esther had to look away. She concentrated instead on Pa's breaths floating toward her on the icy air in cloud-like puffs. She would not give in to temptation. She would not. She had something very special in mind for her treat.

When they arrived home, Esther sprang from the sleigh as soon as it stopped, and raced ahead of Violet and Walter. She found Ma at the kitchen table, cutting carrots into tiny pieces for stew. When she saw Esther,

Ma smiled, but she asked, "Where are your brother and sister?"

"They're coming," Esther answered, wishing that Ma could be happy to see Esther without wanting Walter and Violet. Wasn't Esther alone special enough? Already Ma's eyes had gone back to the straggly carrot she was chopping. But Esther was about to change that.

She walked quickly to the table. "Here, Ma," she said, thrusting her cookie between Ma and the carrot. "Mrs. Davies gave this to me, but I want you to have it."

Ma's eyebrows went up. She smiled kindly at Esther, but she shook her head. "That is your treat, Esther. You must keep it."

"I want you to have it," Esther insisted. "It's my Christmas gift to you."

Ma looked at Esther for a long moment. Finally she nodded. "Thank you, Esther. You are a good-hearted girl." She tucked the cookie in her apron pocket. "The whole family will enjoy this treat on Christmas."

Esther was warmed by Ma's praise. She was less happy about Ma's plan to share the treat Esther had given her—*Esther's* treat—with Walter and Violet, who were at that very moment enjoying theirs. Still, she managed to smile at Ma.

The next day was Christmas Eve, but chores had to be done as usual. After breakfast, Ma even assigned a few extra. She sent Violet and Walter to carry wood to the porch. And she told Esther to clean the kerosene lanterns. Much as Esther disliked the tedious task, that day she made it fun. She pretended she was a good fairy turning ordinary glass into shining diamonds.

After lunch, Pa disappeared. A little while later there was a thumping on the side porch and the parlor door banged open. The top of a fir tree plunged into the room.

"A Christmas tree!" Walter shrieked, leaping up from the floor where he'd been playing.

"Oh, Pa, it's beautiful!" Esther said.

"I knew Pa wouldn't let us have Christmas without a tree," Violet declared, clapping her hands.

Pa smiled at their excitement. "Now where is that star, Walter?" he asked, carrying the tree all the way inside and shutting the door with his foot to keep the cold out.

Walter ran for the star. Ma brought out the box of red and silver balls. Soon everyone was crowded around the tree, hanging the pretty ornaments on its branches. When the last ball was hung, Pa lifted Walter so he could perch the star on top.

"Now it feels like Christmas!" Esther said. Of course, there were no presents to put beneath the pretty fir. There were no cookies cooling in the kitchen. There was no turkey for the dinner, and no family was expected. Still, the tree was a reminder that it really was Christmas, even if it was a much poorer one than usual.

Ma suddenly noticed the time. *"Nu!"* she said. "It is getting late. We must hurry with our baths."

Esther ran for the tub. Special evening services were being held at church and it wouldn't do to be late. But Ma need not have worried. They arrived in plenty of time.

"Oh, look!" Esther whispered when they walked in the front door. "Candles!" They were everywhere, flickering in windows and all around the pulpit. They cast an almost magical glow over the church.

When Reverend Phillips read the Christmas story, Esther felt a thrill she'd never felt before. Up until then, when she thought of Jesus, she thought of him as a man in a white robe, working miracles. That night, for the first time, she thought of him as a real baby—like Henry Christian. She imagined him crying and being comforted by Mary. And she pictured Jesus as a little boy, following Joseph around just like Walter followed Pa. That Christmas Eve, in that little country church, Jesus became real to Esther.

"Merry Christmas!" everyone called to one another afterward. "Merry Christmas!" The joy-filled greeting seemed to float and echo on the crisp night air, following them all the way home.

When they got to the farm, Pa carried a sleepy Walter upstairs. Ma gave the girls each a towel-wrapped brick that had been warming in the oven. Then she shooed them up to bed, too. It was late. Esther undressed and got under the covers, stretched cold toes toward the brick's heat, and drifted off to sleep.

"Merry Christmas! Merry Christmas!" It was Pa's voice.

Esther and Violet sat up, blinking sleepily at each other. Then Walter shot out of his room. Esther jumped up and Violet pounded down the stairs after them both. Halfway down, Esther smelled something she hadn't smelled in a long time. Bacon! Her mouth watered.

"Presents!" she heard Walter yell. "Santa came! Santa came!"

Esther flew down the last stairs to the parlor. She sucked in a breath. Walter was right! Last night the floor beneath the tree had been bare. Now several gaily wrapped packages were there. Esther's heart thudded with anticipation. "Can we open them?" she asked.

"Open, open!" Pa said, waving his hands and smiling. Ma came out of the kitchen to watch as Esther and Violet and Walter knelt by the tree.

"To Esther from Julia," Esther read one tag. She tore open the paper. A book! On the shiny jacket was a picture of a pretty young woman dressed in blue and carrying a clock under her arm. *The Secret of the Old Clock!* Esther told Violet. "It's a mystery book, like the Hardy Boys book Shirley lent me." Inside the cover Julia had written, *This Nancy Drew series is brand-new and supposed to be very good. Merry Christmas! Love, Julia.*

Violet was too excited about her sketch pad and drawing pencils to do more than nod at Esther. Walter was roaring a red truck across the floor. But there were two more presents for Esther to open. Two pretty pink barrettes were from Kate and Howard. And a red, hand-knitted sweater was from Ma and Pa.

"It's beautiful! Thank you, Ma. Thank you, Pa." Esther put down her barrettes and book long enough to slip her arms into the sleeves of the sweater. "Ooooh," she said. "It's nice and warm!"

Esther took a moment to admire the truck Julia had sent to Walter, the tiny train set he'd gotten from Kate and Howard, and the wood farm animals that Santa had brought him. He and Violet had both gotten new sweaters, too. Walter's was brown and Violet's was green. And, just like Esther, Violet had pretty new barrettes. Only hers were sky blue.

"Breakfast," Ma announced, and everyone hurried to the table for potato pancakes with raspberry jam and two strips of bacon each. Esther couldn't remember the last time she'd had such a breakfast! She ate and ate until her stomach was too full for even one more bite.

After breakfast there were chores to do. The animals had to be fed and the cows had to be milked even on Christmas. But afterward Pa played old maid and rummy and go fish with Esther and Violet and Walter, so the morning flew by. A bowl of soup for lunch was just right. Everyone was still full from breakfast, and good smells were already wafting from the stove, promising even better things for supper.

The afternoon was quieter. Pa played checkers with Walter, whistling softly all the while. Violet tried out her sketch pad and pencils. Esther curled up with her mystery story. First, she looked at the exciting black-and-white picture at the front of the book. Then she turned to chapter 1, promising herself to read very slowly so the story would not end too soon.

Dinner was simple compared with past Christmas dinners, but it was a feast to them. Roast chicken with onion stuffing, carrots, potatoes, and biscuits. They ate every morsel. Ma didn't have enough flour to bake a pie or a cake for dessert, but she brought out a special gift from Kate and Howard and little Henry. A small box of chocolate-covered cherries! Esther bit a tiny hole in the side of hers and sucked out the cream filling first. Then she sucked on the chocolate. Last of all she ate the cherry.

"Wonderful, Anna." Pa patted his stomach. "A delicious dinner."

Esther and the others nodded. "Delicious, Ma."

Ma's cheeks turned pink. She jumped up to clear the table.

That night they played rummy again, and this time Ma played with them. She won even more often than Pa! Finally Pa put away the cards to sing Christmas carols in German. "O Tannenbaum" was Esther's favorite. She sang along on the words she knew and hummed on the ones she didn't.

Midway through the singing, Ma went to the kitchen. When she returned, she was carrying the gingerbread man Esther had given her. Esther had forgotten all about it! Ma gave the cookie to Pa and he broke off an arm for Walter and the other one for Violet. Then he broke off a leg for himself and for Ma. Seeing the looks of delight on her brother's and sister's faces made Esther glad that Ma was sharing her treat. Finally, Pa handed the biggest piece of all—the head and body—to Esther. "For the little girl who remembered that Christmas is about sharing with the ones you love," he said.

Ma nodded her agreement, and the pride on her and Pa's faces was like one last and very special gift of the day.

Esther curled up on one end of the sofa to eat her cookie and listen to Pa sing Christmas carols in German. The gingerbread was as sweet to Esther's tongue as Pa's voice was to her ears. She sighed contentedly and wished Christmas Day never had to end.

13 Two Kinds of Luck

ESTHER WASHED HER FACE AND REACHED
for the towel. An instant before she put it to her face,
she saw the spider that was crawling on it. She let out a
startled squeal, threw down the towel, and stomped on
the spider, squashing it under her shoe.

Ma, hearing her squeal, turned around just in time to
see the spider meet its death. Her face went red. "Why
did you do that?" she demanded. "To see a spider before
breakfast is good luck! This family could use some good
luck for a change."

Esther cringed. Ma was so angry. "I'm sorry, Ma. I was
so scared, I didn't think."

"You must *start* to think!" Ma said. Then she shook her
head and turned away.

Esther bit her lip. She couldn't seem to do anything right lately. Not that Walter or Violet were faring much better. It took little to trigger Ma's temper these days—a lamp left burning, a door closed too slowly, a crumb of food dropped.

The New Year had begun badly and gotten steadily worse. Bitterly cold weather forced them to burn more wood than ever. And the animals ate more food to keep warm. With the woodpile dwindling, the animals' feed going fast, and their own supplies nearly gone, Pa had tried desperately to find work. But no one in any of the nearby towns was hiring. Each time he returned home, his steps were heavier, his back was more bowed.

Pa came in from the barn as Esther was hanging a fresh towel at the sink. He thumped a crock of milk onto the table. "There's not enough to sell," he told Ma. "Let the children drink."

So Esther had milk for the first time in weeks. She'd never realized before how good it tasted. Walter must have thought so, too. He drank down his glass in noisy gulps.

"Walter!" Ma scolded.

He ducked his head but flashed a milk-framed grin at Esther when Ma left the table.

Pa drove them to school in the sleigh that day as usual. But his face was solemn when he waved good-bye. Esther's heart ached to see him so sad and silent. She hadn't heard him whistle since Christmas. She hadn't seen him smile in days. She wished there was something she could do to make him happy again. But she couldn't think what that might be. She trudged up the snowy path to the schoolhouse.

"Esther!"

Esther looked up to see Bethany waving from the schoolhouse steps. "Hurry! The cast list is posted!" Bethany yelled.

Esther needed no further prompting. At last they'd find out their parts in the play. She raced past Violet and Walter. "Have you looked yet?" she asked Bethany breathlessly.

Bethany shook her head. "I wanted to wait for you."

"Well, here I am," Esther said with a nervous laugh, remembering the lucky spider she had killed. "Let's go see."

Holding hands, they hurried inside. There was a cluster of students at the back of their classroom. Bethany and Esther wriggled and nudged their way through them. Esther held her breath and squeezed Bethany's hand tight as she squinted up at the list on the wall. But Bethany saw Esther's name before she did.

"You're one of the princesses, Esther!" she said. "You're one of the *princesses!*"

Esther's heart gave a leap. "Really? *Really?*" She pushed a little closer so she could see where Bethany was pointing. Sure enough, it said *Youngest princess: Esther Vogel.* Esther felt her mouth stretching into a grin. Then she remembered Bethany. "What part did you get?"

Bethany shrugged. "I'm a kitchen maid. But I didn't expect a big part. I can't memorize things the way you can, and the fifth-graders always get the small roles. Except for you," she said, shaking her head in admiration. "You're the only fifth-grader to get a starring role."

Esther's cheeks warmed. She was pleased but a little embarrassed, too. When she was jostled from behind, she used it as an excuse to change the subject. "Let's get out of here before we're trampled." They walked back out to the hallway to hang up their coats. "Did you finish knitting your sweater yet?" she asked.

For answer Bethany slipped off her coat and revealed a rose-colored cardigan.

"Oh, Bethany!" Esther gasped. "It's beautiful. I don't know how you had the patience to do it. I'm all thumbs whenever I try to knit. I couldn't even finish the little scarf I started for Margaret."

It was Bethany's turn to blush. "Mama helped me a little," she confided. "Especially setting the sleeves."

"Ten mothers could help me. I still couldn't begin to make something so fine," Esther said. Giggling, they went back to the classroom.

When Pa picked them up after school, Esther was quick to tell him about her part in the play. He nodded. "Good. Good." But otherwise he was silent. It was a cold day. Esther gave up talking and burrowed into the straw Pa had piled in the sleigh. It was a little prickly, but it kept the worst of the cold and wind out.

At home, Esther and Violet set their books on the kitchen table. Pa walked past them to the parlor. When he came back, he had the radio in his arms. All these months it had sat silently but proudly on the little table in the parlor. It had comforted Esther to see it sitting there like a promise of better things to come. But now Pa was taking it away.

"Where are you taking the radio, Pa?" she asked quickly.

"To sell it," Pa replied. "There is a shop in Middleton that will pay a good price."

Esther and Violet looked at each other in dismay. Esther wanted to beg Pa not to do it. But there was a look on Pa's face that made her keep silent. He strode past them and out the door. Ma never said a word. She did not even look up from the carrots she was scraping at the sink.

When he came home later, Pa's back was very straight. His head was high. He nodded to Ma. "Make a list of what you need. I will take it with me tomorrow morning."

Ma nodded. There was a look of satisfaction on her face.

Then Pa sat down. He scooped Walter up and bounced him on his knee.

Esther was glad to see the frown was gone from Pa's face. But she was sad to think of the price he'd had to pay to remove it. The radio had been so important to him!

Suddenly Esther cast a sharp look at Ma. She had never liked the radio. Maybe she had thought this would be a good way to get rid of it. Maybe she'd made Pa feel guilty for having something that wasn't useful now and might never be again. Maybe she made him feel he *had* to sell it.

Esther could easily imagine Ma doing these things, especially lately. She felt a flash of anger as she recalled Ma's satisfied nod. How would Ma feel if Pa had sold her sewing machine?

But angry as she was, Esther knew it wouldn't be the same. The sewing machine didn't need electricity to work. And even if it had, it still would have been useful someday for making their clothing and curtains. The radio was only for pleasure. Still, it seemed as if there should've been something else he could have sold. Her gaze swept through the downstairs of the farmhouse— but there were just simple pieces of furniture, things they really needed.

There was nothing so fine—and so unnecessary—as the radio had been.

Esther sighed. It probably was wrong to blame Ma. She was just worried because their food supplies were running low. Still, Esther thought it would be easier to bear the loss of the radio if she thought Ma was sad about it, too. And there was no way to tell about something like that with Ma.

"Now, Esther, tell me about this play," Pa said. "What are you and Violet to be?"

"I'm going to be a princess, Pa," Esther said proudly. "The youngest one. I get lots of lines to say."

"And I'm going to be a lady-in-waiting," Violet told him happily. "I get to wear a pretty dress and I don't have to say hardly anything at all."

While they were talking at the table, Ma was at the stove. She was making soup. When it was time for supper, she placed a steaming bowlful in front of each of them. Esther dipped her spoon into it hungrily. The soup was more water than vegetables and had no potatoes or meat. Still, it filled the groaning hollow inside her.

"Can I have some bread, Ma?" Walter asked.

Ma sat down and picked up her spoon. "There is no bread," she said quietly.

Esther's head snapped up in surprise. No bread? Her heart fluttered strangely. She looked from Ma to Pa and back again. But they didn't look up from their soup. Esther's stomach twisted painfully. Things were much worse than she had thought. It wasn't just that their food was running low. Their food was gone! That must be why Ma had not sent her to the cellar lately. She didn't want Esther to see how little was there. But now she knew.

And even the hot soup could not melt the icy lump in her stomach.

No wonder Pa had sold the radio. And no wonder Ma had looked pleased. Esther's cheeks were hot. But not from the heat of the soup—from shame at having such mean thoughts about Ma.

That night in bed, Esther huddled close to Violet. She pulled the quilt up around her ears. It had been so cold lately that Ma had taken to putting extra bricks under the covers before bedtime. The sheets and quilts were warm around Esther's shoulders now, even though the bricks were gone. Mmmm. She turned over and snuggled into her pillow with Margaret cradled in her arm.

Suddenly she remembered the spider she'd killed that morning. Had it brought bad luck or good? She had gotten a big part in the play, so that was good. But Pa had sold the radio, and that was very bad. Pa had seemed happier, though, and there would be food now.

Esther frowned in the darkness. It was confusing. As if good luck and bad luck were all tangled together. She sighed. She wasn't sure of anything—except the next time she saw a spider before breakfast, she was going to leave it be.

14 What Ma Did

THE MONEY FROM SELLING THE RADIO made things better for a while. It bought a big bag of flour, a bushel of potatoes, some oatmeal, cheese, and beans. It even bought a precious bit of beef Ma used to flavor countless pots of soup. But as February came to an end, their supplies were once again dwindling. Potatoes and carrots in weak broth were suppers most nights. Bread was cut back to a slice at lunchtime only. Thin oatmeal was breakfast. Walter's rosy cheeks had grown pale. Esther's face looked pinched in the mirror. Ma's dresses hung loosely on her.

Pa sold one of the cows. It was the only way he could

buy feed for the other animals, but he hadn't smiled since.

Esther shivered and buttoned her Christmas sweater to her chin. Even at the kitchen table it was cold. Ma fed the stove and fireplace just enough wood to keep their fires going.

February 27, 1931

Dear Julia,

It gets very cold in Wisconsin in the winter. All our windows are so covered with frost, we cannot see out. Mickey sleeps in the barn now because it is too cold under the porch. He runs out as soon as Pa opens the barn door, though, so he is always waiting for me in the morning. It has not snowed much lately. I am glad. If it did, we might not be able to go to school. We would miss rehearsals for our spring play.

Esther stopped. Writing letters wasn't as much fun as it used to be. Her fingers were icy and stiff. And there were too many things Ma and Pa didn't want her to write about.

"Do not tell them I sold the radio," Pa told her.

"Do not complain that you are hungry or cold," Ma told her.

It seemed to Esther that hungry and cold were all

there was—at home, anyway. That meant school was all she could write about. She nibbled on the end of her pencil for a moment and then wrote:

Bethany says I am a born actress. She says everyone else looks like wooden puppets next to me. I always thought I would be a teacher when I grow up. Now I think maybe I will be an actress.

Esther closed her eyes and imagined herself on a stage with hundreds of people applauding and cheering. She bowed low. And when she straightened, she saw Ma and Pa sitting in the front row. They were clapping, too. Ma's eyes were shining and she was clapping hardest of all . . .

Esther heard the whisper of Ma's iron sliding across fabric. She looked up and watched Ma iron the back of Pa's shirt with long, smooth motions. Abruptly Ma turned and set the iron on the stove top. It had cooled. She unfastened the handle and snapped it onto one of the other irons that were heating on the stove. Then the iron whispered again.

Esther put down her pencil and rubbed her hands together. Enough. It was too cold to write today. She took her letter upstairs and brought Margaret down instead. They would have a tea party on the floor in front of the fireplace.

In a few minutes Esther was warmer. She held her

pretend teacup and smiled at Margaret. "I hope you're feeling well." Margaret smiled back. She was very well indeed.

Ma interrupted the tea party to tell Esther, "Watch supper. Walter and I are going to bring in more wood. If Violet wants tea, there's hot water in the kettle."

Esther nodded. Violet had a terrible cold. She'd been coughing and sniffling for days. She was resting in Ma and Pa's bed because it was warmer than upstairs. "Yes, Ma."

Ma and Walter wrapped themselves in coats and scarves and went out. Esther's tea party continued. "More lemon?" she asked Margaret.

She and Margaret were in the middle of a conversation about their favorite books when the door slammed. "*Nu!* Esther!"

Esther nearly choked on her pretend tea. She scrambled to her feet. Instantly she smelled something burning. Supper! Horror stricken, she ran into the kitchen just in time to see Ma yank open the oven door. A cloud of smoke billowed out. The pan of beans she pulled out was charred black.

Ma hurled the pan into the sink. It landed with a crash. Then she turned on Esther. "I told you to vatch supper," she said. "Instead you let it burn to cinders."

"I'm s-sorry, Ma," Esther said. "I forgot. I was playing and—"

"Playing, yes!" Ma nodded. "Vith your doll. You, a big girl of almost eleven!" Ma's eyes blazed. "*Nu!* Bring me the doll."

Esther went on trembling legs and gathered Margaret in her arms. She had never seen Ma so angry—not even the day she'd found out that Esther was still friends with Bethany. Then her anger had been mixed with sadness. This time it was anger through and through. What was she going to do with Margaret? Full of dread, Esther carried her doll back into the kitchen. "Please," she begged. "I'm sorry. Don't—"

But Ma had already torn Margaret from Esther's grasp. She turned and flung the doll into the garbage pail. "There!" she said. "Next time you vill do as you are told."

"No!" Esther wailed. But a fierce look silenced her.

"Go get three potatoes from the cellar," Ma ordered.

Blinded by tears, Esther stumbled down the ladder to obey.

Later, when Ma was checking on Violet, Esther dared to take one last look at Margaret. She dug frantically through charred beans and beets Ma had thrown away because the jar had gone bad. Finally her fingers touched a rounded arm. She grasped it, pulled, and immediately wished she had not.

There was Margaret, but not the beautiful Margaret Esther had known. This was an ugly, ruined

Margaret. Her golden hair was dripping with beet juice. Her once cream-white face was streaked and spotted with horrible brown and red stains. Clumps of burned beans clung to her smudged and spattered dress. And she smelled, sickeningly, of spoiled beets.

"Oh, Margaret!" Esther sobbed. Gently she returned the doll to the garbage. Her heart ached. Her eyes burned with hot tears. What would she do without Margaret? Who would she tell her secrets to? Who would she share her dreams with and confide her fears to?

That night, Esther soaked her pillow with wave after wave of tears.

"I'm sorry, Es." Violet sniffled beside her. "I know you miss her."

Esther was grateful for Violet's sympathy, but she longed for Julia. Without Margaret, she missed Julia more than ever. She could have told Julia that she was crying for even more than the loss of Margaret. Julia would have understood. But practical, down-to-earth Violet never would. And Julia was far, far away.

So Esther had to hug the terrible truth to herself. She had to face it and accept it once and for all—a truth that no amount of wishing or words or hard work would ever change. It wasn't just that Ma didn't love Esther as much as she loved her other children. Ma did not love Esther at *all*. If she did, she could never have done what she'd done to Margaret.

The next day was Saturday, which meant no escaping to school. Esther did her chores silently, ate her oatmeal silently. Then she slipped away to her room and shivered. She would not stay downstairs near Ma. Whenever Esther looked at her, she remembered the fury on Ma's face when she'd hurled Margaret into the garbage. It made the cold lump of hurt and anger in Esther's chest grow bigger. Mrs. Rubinstein would never have looked at Shirley that way! No mother who loved her daughter would.

The cold lump in her chest swelled until Esther could barely breathe in Ma's presence. It only eased—and then just a little—when she was alone in her room.

When the pain in her stomach began, Esther was sure it would go away in a while. She blamed it on the oatmeal, which had been even thinner than usual. She wrapped herself in a blanket and opened *The Secret of the Old Clock*. But she'd only read a few pages when the pain got worse. The book slipped from her fingers. She rolled onto her side and hugged her stomach.

When Walter came to tell her it was lunchtime, she told him, "I'm not hungry." She half expected Ma to come up and insist that she eat something. And, truth to tell, she was almost disappointed when Ma did not. The pain had gotten worse. It was sharper and stronger. It was so bad, she felt like she was going to—

Esther rolled from the bed and got to the chamber pot

just in time. Up came her breakfast. That should have made her feel better. But her stomach hurt worse than ever. Hunched over and fighting back tears, Esther made her way down the stairs. She shuffled into the kitchen, where Ma was just finishing the dishes.

"Ma," Esther said weakly. "I don't feel good."

Ma took one look at Esther and hurried across the room. "Come," she said, guiding Esther to the parlor. "Lie down on the couch. What is wrong? Tell me."

"My stomach, Ma. It hurts. It hurts real bad—here." Esther pointed to her right side. "I threw up."

Ma nodded, her hand on Esther's forehead. Her eyes widened. "You are hot," she said. "Vait here." She scurried into the kitchen and came back with a cold wet cloth for Esther's forehead. "Walter! Go to the barn. Get Pa. Hurry!"

The urgency in her voice alarmed Esther. "What's wrong, Ma?"

"Sssshhh," Ma said. "Do not vorry."

Suddenly Esther tugged at Ma's sleeve. "I'm going to be sick—"

Ma held Esther while she threw up on the parlor floor.

"I'm sorry, Ma," Esther said afterward, ashamed of the mess she'd made. "I didn't know it was coming."

But Ma was not angry. "It does not matter. It is all right," she said, wiping Esther's face gently with the wet cloth. Then Ma settled Esther back on the couch and cleaned up the floor.

She was just finishing when Pa burst into the kitchen. Ma jumped up. "Go get Brummel," she told Pa. "He must drive us to a hospital."

Hospital! Esther tried to sit up, but the pain was too sharp.

"Hospital?" said Pa. He frowned. "What is it? What is wrong with her?"

"I think it is her appendix," Ma said. "Lucy Gould's daughter had the same fever and pain and sickness. They had to take her appendix out. Go, quickly!"

Pa didn't say another word. He ran out the door. A minute later Esther heard one of the horses gallop past. Ma brought a bucket and a fresh cold cloth. She sat on the sofa next to Esther and pressed the cloth to her hot face.

"I'm scared, Ma," Esther whimpered. "I don't want to go to the hospital."

"Do not be afraid," Ma said softly. "They vill make you better. You vill see."

Esther was sick in the bucket two more times before Pa returned. Each time Ma held her head and soothed her with gentle murmurs. Many times she spoke in Russian. Esther couldn't understand the words, but she knew they were words meant to comfort her. She could tell by the way Ma said them. She could tell by the soft look on Ma's face.

All the while the pain kept getting worse. Until

Esther was glad to be going to the hospital. She was frightened by the horrible pain. She was worn out by it. She just wanted it to stop.

"Brummel's outside," Pa said, charging through the kitchen door. "I'll get her coat."

"Never mind a coat," Ma said. "Wrap her in this." She had the quilt from her and Pa's bed. Together she and Pa bundled and tucked it around Esther.

From her patchwork cocoon, Esther caught a glimpse of Violet holding Walter's hand. Their faces were white. Their eyes were big and frightened. Then Pa gathered her in his arms. He pulled a corner of the quilt down to cover her face and he carried her outside. When Ma pulled the quilt back from Esther's face a minute later, they were in the back of Mr. Brummel's car. Esther was lying across the seat. Her head was resting in Ma's lap.

"Don't you worry none, little girl," Mr. Brummel said over his shoulder to Esther. "I'll get you to Madison in no time."

The car went fast, but the pain grew stronger fast, too. Esther couldn't hold back a moan. She saw Ma wince and felt her cool hand on her forehead. "I know it hurts," Ma said. "Be brave just a little longer. Soon ve vill be there."

Esther tried to be brave, like Ma when she sprained her ankle, but the pain bored into her. No matter how she tried to wrap herself around it, or how she tried to pull away from it, it would not let her go. A tear trickled down her cheek. She hoped Ma would not see it. Tears always made her angry. But not this time.

"Ahh," Ma moaned when she saw the tear. Then she gently wiped it away with her thumb. In spite of her pain, Esther felt a flash of comfort. Could she have been wrong about Ma? Did she perhaps love Esther a little after all?

But the pain bored deeper still. Esther could not think anymore. She could only feel. Pain. She thrashed out at it. She squirmed and cried out and tried to run away from it. Each time Ma's hands stilled her. Ma's voice soothed her. Until the pain carried Esther away again.

Esther felt the car lurch to a stop. Cold air swam past her cheeks. She blinked in confusion. The car doors were flung open. Pa scooped her up and ran through a doorway. People in white came running. They were at the hospital.

A doctor with kind eyes and gentle hands swiftly examined Esther. "That appendix is ready to burst," he said. "It's got to come out and fast."

Ma and Pa were hovering just behind him. Esther saw them nod. "Yes, do the operation! Just make her well."

Suddenly Esther was terrified. "Ma! Pa!" she sobbed.

Pa hugged her and kissed her cheek. Ma held Esther's hand tight and murmured soft Russian words into Esther's ear. Then the doctor made them step back. Esther was rolled away down a bright hallway into a brighter room.

A nice nurse held her hand. A man with a white mask covering his nose and mouth told Esther, "Just breathe normally, sweetheart, and you'll be off to dreamland before you know it." Something that smelled nasty-sweet was pressed against her nose. Esther tried to turn her face away, but she couldn't. She had to breathe in the smell. From somewhere came the thought that at least it wasn't as bad as the pigsty. Then Esther floated into a swirling tunnel of darkness . . .

When Esther woke up, the first thing she saw was Ma's face. It was dark behind Ma, but her face was lit by a small lamp on the table next to Esther's bed.

"Ahh. You are awake finally," Ma said. She smiled.

"Thir . . . sty," Esther croaked.

"I will get some water," Ma said. "Wait." Esther closed her eyes and listened to Ma's footsteps fade away. When she heard them coming back, Esther forced her heavy eyelids to open again. Ma held a cup with a spoon sticking out of it. "Ice chips," she said, spooning one carefully into Esther's mouth.

Esther closed her eyes. The ice tasted wonderful. When it was gone, she asked, "Where's Pa?"

"He stayed until the doctor said you were out of danger," Ma said. "He said good-bye to you. But he had to go back with Brummel. He had to see to the animals and Violet and Walter. He will come again tomorrow."

Esther nodded weakly. "Is my operation over?" she asked.

Ma nodded. "Yes. All over. You will be fine."

"Good," Esther whispered. Then she fell asleep again.

The next time she woke up, a voice was saying, "She needs plenty of good food and rest."

"We will see that she gets them," Ma said.

"She's very weak," the voice continued. "Aside from the surgery, she's half starved."

Ma's voice hardened. "I understand. But she will get everything she needs." She added more softly, "I promise."

Esther's eyes opened but the room was dark. She couldn't see Ma or the man she was talking to. She tried to turn to look toward the doorway. But pain sliced through her middle. "Ooooh!" she gasped.

Ma was at her side in an instant. The lamp snapped on. "What is it? What is wrong?"

"It hurts," Esther moaned, squinting in the glare of the light.

A man dressed in white came and stood beside Ma. He smiled down at Esther. She recognized him then. He was the same doctor who had examined her when she arrived at the hospital. "It's going to hurt for a while, I'm afraid," he said. "But not so bad as it hurt before, hmm?"

Esther shook her head. No, not so bad as that. And if she lay very still, not so bad at all.

"The nurse will give you medicine for the pain," the

doctor said. "And in a few days you'll feel more like your-self. You'll see."

"Then can I go home?" Esther asked anxiously. She didn't want to hurt the doctor's feelings. He and everyone else at the hospital had been very nice. But she didn't really like it there. She wanted to go home to the farm and be with Ma and Pa and Violet and Walter and Mickey.

Ma and the doctor looked at each other and quickly away.

"Already in a hurry to leave, are you?" the doctor joked. "Wait 'til you taste the food." He patted her hand. "Just rest now. You'll go home when you're stronger."

It wasn't the answer Esther wanted, but the little bit of talking had tired her. She sighed and closed her eyes. If she couldn't really be home, she would pretend. She would pretend she was in her own bed with Violet beside her. Walter was in the room next door, and Ma and Pa were downstairs. Mickey was sleeping in the barn where it was warm, curled up near Bruno and Fritz. And the cows were dozing nearby.

Half asleep and muddled, Esther wondered why Ma was holding her hand. She should be sleeping downstairs with Pa. But it took too much effort to puzzle it out. It was just nice to feel Ma's hand in hers. It was warm and strong. It made Esther feel safe, as if nothing bad could ever touch her. Ma would not let it.

"I love you."

Someone spoke the words. Was it Ma? Or was it Esther herself? Esther needed to know. She struggled desperately against the heavy darkness that pulled at her. But in the end, exhausted, she gave in and slept.

15 City Girl Again

ESTHER SAT BY THE WINDOW AND STARED down at the street. Boys were playing stickball and two girls were drawing a hopscotch game on the sidewalk with the edge of a stone, the way she and Shirley used to do.

Kate's shadow fell on Esther's lap as she came carrying a dish of custard. "It's hard to watch, I know," Kate said. "But soon you'll be down there playing with them."

Esther took the custard and shrugged. "I don't care really."

Kate's eyebrows shot up. "I'd think after three weeks here and almost two more in that hospital, you'd be itching to get outside again."

Esther was glad little Henry's wake-up whimpers took

Kate speeding away. Kate and Howard and Julia had been so good to her. They had driven up to the hospital to bring her back to Chicago. They had fussed over her and fed her. Julia had even given up her bed. She was sleeping on the sofa so Esther could be comfortable. How could she tell them that all she wanted was to go back to the farm?

She remembered how shocked she'd been when Ma told her she couldn't go home.

"We cannot care for you there," Ma had said. "You know there is hardly any food. And it is so cold. No, you must go to your sisters. It is the only way."

"No!" Esther cried, clutching Ma's arm. "I don't want to. I want to stay with you and Pa. I'll get well, I promise."

But Ma was firm. "It is already arranged. Kate and Howard will come tomorrow. It is best. You will see."

Esther gulped down a sob and sniffled. "For how long?" she asked. "When can I come back home?"

Ma straightened Esther's sheets. "Soon. We will all be together again soon."

But that had been weeks ago, and Esther was still in Chicago. She was impatient to get back. She missed everyone so much—the family, Bethany, Mickey, and Bruno. Soon she'd be so far behind in school that she'd never catch up. She had already missed the spring play. After weeks of rehearsing, someone else had gotten to be the princess. The unfairness of it made Esther's eyes fill with tears. She wiped them away quickly, though, when she heard Julia's footsteps on the stairs.

"Hello, sweetie," Julia greeted her. She gave Esther a big hug even before she took off her coat. "How are you today?"

"All right, I guess," Esther said.

"Just 'all right,' huh?" Julia said. "Then maybe this letter will cheer you up." She waved an envelope addressed in Pa's straight up-and-down script. "Let me just get Kate first—"

"Here I am," Kate said, coming in with Henry in her arms. "Why? What is it?"

"A letter from Pa!" Esther told her. "Read it quick, Julia. Maybe it says I can come home." She leaned forward in her chair. Maybe she could even go home tomorrow. It wouldn't take her long to pack.

Julia slit the envelope and pulled out the single sheet of paper inside. Then she sat back to read.

My Daughters,

It means so much to Ma and me to know you are together and well. We are especially thankful Esther is growing strong and healthy again in your care.

Esther sat up straighter and held her breath. Here was where Pa would say it was time for her to come home again. She wished Julia would read faster!

"It has not been easy," Julia read on, "but Ma and I have decided to sell the farm."

"No!" Esther jumped up from her chair. The dish of custard slid from her lap, fell to the floor, and shattered at her feet. Esther didn't care. She stomped her foot. She shook her head, insisting over and over again, "No! No!"

Julia flew to her side. She put an arm around Esther's shaking shoulders. Gently she steered her past the bits of broken dish and custard. She drew her down onto the sofa beside her. Then, holding Esther tight in the circle of her arm, Julia finished the letter.

The winter was too hard. We have no money left for seed. It is time to go back to the city and try again there. With the sale of the farm we will have enough to rent a small apartment while I look for work. We hope to be there before the end of the month. If you could find an apartment that would do, we would be grateful.

Love,

Pa

"No," Esther whispered. "No." But it was just like the day Pa walked off with the radio under his arm. The decision had already been made. Nothing she could do would change it. She was never going to see the farm again. She was never going to see Bethany or Mickey. They were as lost to her as Margaret. She didn't even try to hold back her sobs.

"Oh, Esther . . . ," Kate said.

Julia held her close and murmured, "Ssshhh. It will be all right."

But Esther knew better. Nothing would be all right. Not ever again.

The next two weeks were miserable ones for Esther. Kate and Julia were sympathetic. But they couldn't help being glad the family would be together again.

"You're going to meet your Vogel grandparents soon," Kate said to Henry half a dozen times a day, it seemed to Esther.

And every day Julia hunched over the *Tribune*, circling advertisements for apartments, until finally she was able to report, "I've found the perfect place. It's just two blocks away, and it's empty. They can move in as soon as they arrive."

She invited Esther to take a walk with her to see it, but Esther shook her head. "I'm tired," she said. Julia patted her shoulder and let her be.

One night, Howard brought a friend home for dinner. Esther thought there was something familiar about the bearded guest. Then Howard introduced the man as Sam Rubinstein. Esther sprang out of her chair.

"Mr. Rubinstein! I remember you. You're Shirley's father," she cried. She was more excited than she'd been in weeks. Shirley was back!

"Yes, I am," Mr. Rubinstein said, reaching out to take her hand in his. "And I remember you, too, now. Little Esther Vogel—Shirley's good friend. How nice that we should meet again."

Esther nodded. It was nice, but it was odd, too. Part of the reason she hadn't recognized Mr. Rubinstein was that she'd never seen him in work clothes before. He'd always worn a suit. And he hadn't had a beard back then, just a neatly trimmed mustache. "I can't wait to see Shirley again," she told him. "I have so much to tell her."

Mr. Rubinstein patted Esther's hand before he let it go. "I only wish that Shirley were here," he said sadly. "I miss her, too."

"But where is she?" Esther asked. "How come she's not with you?"

"Esther," Howard said gently. "You're asking very personal questions."

But Mr. Rubinstein waved a hand at him. "She's entitled to ask. The girls were good friends, then Shirley disappeared without a word. Esther must have done a lot of wondering about her over the past year."

"Well, at least have a seat, Sam," Howard said. "Then you two can talk as much as you like. I'll go help Kate." Howard left the room and Mr. Rubinstein sat on the sofa. He patted the cushion beside him.

"Come and sit with me," he invited. "I miss having a little girl at my side."

Esther sat down next to Mr. Rubinstein. "If Shirley isn't here, where is she?" she dared to ask.

"She's with her mother and her mother's family in Dayton, Ohio," Mr. Rubinstein replied. "When my business failed, it meant a lot of changes for my family, I'm afraid."

"But how come they're not here with you?" Esther asked softly. She was afraid she was being too personal again, but she was confused. Pa lost his job but they had stayed together.

Mr. Rubinstein tugged on the bottom of his beard. "Miriam—Mrs. Rubinstein—has always had a lovely home and every convenience. To suddenly lose it all and be expected to move to some tiny apartment—it was just too difficult for her. She went to live with her parents until things are better." Mr. Rubinstein looked down at his hands. They were red and scarred like Howard's. But they had not always been that way.

"It's for the best," Mr. Rubinstein added, although he didn't sound as if he meant it. "Miriam is happier this way, and Shirley has everything she needs. I see them whenever I can. And someday, when I get back on my feet, we'll be together again." He smiled down at Esther. "I'll tell Shirley I've seen you. She'll have a million questions, too. Tell me what you've been up to."

Esther told him about their move to the farm. She told him about Mickey and Bethany. She told him about feeding the pigs and riding Bruno and running from the geese. She told him about her operation. And finally, she told him that the family was moving back to the city again. "I wish they weren't," she confided. "I loved the farm. I wanted to stay there forever."

Mr. Rubinstein slipped an arm around Esther's shoulders and squeezed. "Part of growing up is accepting things the way they are. Making the best of them instead of always wishing they were different." He took his arm away and nodded. "But I can see you've already learned that."

Howard and Kate came in then and it was time for supper. The grown-ups talked steadily throughout the simple meal. Except for a quick good-bye, Esther didn't talk to Mr. Rubinstein again. But he had given her a lot to think about.

Most of all she thought about Mrs. Rubinstein. How could she have left Mr. Rubinstein all alone just so she could live in a pretty house? Ma would never leave Pa. She didn't leave him even when he took her to a home that had no electricity, no running water, and no bathroom!

The more Esther thought about it, the more upset she became. She had thought Mrs. Rubinstein was so wonderful. She had wished and wished for Ma to be just like her. She had thought Mrs. Rubinstein knew all about loving. It wasn't just Shirley she had hugged and kissed. She'd greeted Mr. Rubinstein that way, too. But then she had left him all alone, just so her life would stay fine and easy. That wasn't Esther's idea of love. How could I have been so wrong? she asked herself over and over again.

She thought about what Mr. Rubinstein had said—that growing up meant accepting things the way they were. It meant not complaining all the time because things weren't what you wanted. He'd said he could see she had already learned that.

But Esther wasn't so sure. She certainly hadn't accepted Ma the way she was. She'd spent a whole year trying to change her—all so she would know for sure that Ma loved her. Esther had wanted to hear the words. She had wanted the hugs and the kisses. And now she realized they didn't mean love at all.

What was love, then? How was a person supposed to recognize it? Esther got ready for bed very slowly. Thoughts were twirling around and bumping into one another in her head. Esther could not get a firm grasp on any of them.

She wished Julia were there. No doubt she would be able to sort out Esther's confusion. But Julia was working the night shift that week. She slept when Esther was awake, and scurried off to the telephone company when she woke up. There would be no real time to talk until the weekend.

Saturday finally came. That was Julia's day off. It was also the day Ma and Pa and Violet and Walter were coming back to Chicago. Howard had left long before dawn to get them. In spite of her sadness over losing the farm, Esther was excited by the thought that she would be with her family before the day ended. She even laughed when Henry crawled inside a cardboard box Kate had left sitting on the floor. Kate lifted him out and gave him a pot and spoon instead. Julia put the box on the table, where she packed it with food while Esther watched.

"It's just a few things to get you all started," Julia said. She set a bag of sugar next to a bag of flour. Then she added a loaf of fresh-baked bread, a box of salt, some bacon, a chunk of cheese, a smaller chunk of butter, a jar of applesauce, and a dozen eggs. "There."

Seeing the eggs reminded Esther. "I used to gather the eggs on the farm. One hen was so mean, she'd try to peck me."

Julia smiled. "Your life was very different there."

Esther nodded. "Yes. But mostly in nice ways."

Julia folded the flaps of the box down, closing its top. "I'm taking this over to put away before they arrive," she said. "Want to come along?"

Esther hesitated. Not going to the apartment didn't change the fact that she was going to live there instead of the farm. She nodded. "All right."

They left Kate frosting a cake she'd baked for that night's special supper. Henry was playing with the pot and spoon on the floor nearby. "See you later," Esther called over his banging.

It was a beautiful April day. The sun was shining in a bright blue sky and the temperature was warm. Esther lifted her face to the sun and took a slow, deep breath. It was good to be outside again. And it was the perfect opportunity to talk to Julia. She could ask her questions about love.

But Esther just walked silently at Julia's side. She realized suddenly that she didn't want Julia's answers. She wanted to find her own. And something inside her was telling her she was very close now. Her thoughts were like seeds planted and sprouting in dark soil. Esther could feel them growing, working their way to the surface. She just had to be patient. Like Pa had been patient when he'd waited for the crops to grow.

Julia stopped at a green painted door. It was next to a barbershop with a red-and-white-striped pole out front. The red-striped pole next to the green door made Esther think of Christmas. Last Christmas had been such a happy time. She smiled. She would always have memories of her happy times on the farm. No one could take them away.

Julia opened the door and led the way upstairs to the apartment above the barbershop. Esther sniffed. The hallway smelled of spicy shaving cream and hair pomade.

Pleasant smells to come home to. Not like Mrs. Pulaski's stinky sauerkraut at their old apartment building. Ugh!

Julia set down her box and took a key from her skirt pocket. She was about to put it in the door when she stopped and offered it to Esther.

"Why don't you do the honors?" she said, stepping aside.

Esther slid the key into the lock and turned it. Then she led the way inside. It was smaller than their old apartment, and darker. But it had freshly painted walls, and the linoleum in the kitchen was new enough that it still had some shine left. Esther's footsteps echoed as she walked through the empty rooms—the parlor, the kitchen, two bedrooms, and one bathroom.

When Esther came to the bathroom, she grinned. "Violet will probably want to live in here," she said.

"There's a little porch, too," Julia said, leading the way to the back door and opening it.

Esther looked. There was a porch all right. The perfect place for a dog to curl up and nap in the shade on a summer afternoon. Oh, if only Mickey could come, too! But Esther knew Ma would never agree to a dog in the city. And Esther also knew that Mickey would never be truly happy here. He was used to running free through the fields.

But who would love him now? Would the new owners be kind to him? She would never know.

Esther closed the door harder than she should have. The noise startled Julia. She jumped, knocking over the box of salt she'd just unpacked.

"Oops—sorry," Esther said.

"No harm done," Julia said. "Just a little spilled salt, easily taken care of." She brushed the salt into her hand and tossed it over her left shoulder into the sink.

"Why did you do that?" Esther asked quickly. "Throw the salt over your shoulder, I mean."

Julia blushed. "For luck. *You* know."

"I know that spilling salt is supposed to be bad luck," Esther said. "And I know tossing it over your left shoulder is supposed to undo it. But do you really believe it?" She stared at Julia hard, waiting for her answer.

Julia ducked her head and grinned. "Not really. But I do it anyway because it's what Ma taught me. I do it . . . just in case." She looked embarrassed. So she didn't really believe in superstitions. But she was afraid to ignore them "just in case" she was wrong.

Esther suddenly remembered how she used to walk to school in the city. She'd always been careful not to step on the cracks in the sidewalk. "Step on a crack, break your mother's back" was what everyone said. And she'd been afraid to take any chances, even though she was sure it couldn't be so. After all, many children walked the same sidewalk every day and stepped on cracks lots of times. Surely all their mothers had not broken their backs!

But maybe some things didn't have to make sense for people to believe in them. Maybe—like Julia—most people thought it was better to be careful than to take a chance. But what about the others?

"Bethany's family doesn't believe in superstitions," Esther told Julia. "They even have a black cat!"

"Really?" Julia said. "That's brave of them."

"No-o-o-o-o," Esther replied slowly, some of her confusion beginning to come clear. "Because they aren't afraid. They don't worry about bad things happening, and bad things mostly don't."

Esther thought of the wonderful afternoon she had spent on the Klause farm. She remembered how Mr. Klause had teased her and Bethany, and how Mrs. Klause had kissed baby Rose's cheek and declared her the sweetest baby in Wisconsin.

"They were the happiest family I've ever known," Esther said.

"Mmmm," Julia said, putting the eggs and butter in the icebox. "I'm glad you had such a nice girl for a friend."

Esther nodded. "Me too."

Ma and Pa arrived a few minutes later, just as Esther and Julia were leaving.

"You're early!" Julia squealed. "Welcome home!" She fell on Ma and Pa and Violet and Walter even before they were through the door. Esther, suddenly shy, hung back.

"Howard went to return the car. He will be back

soon," Pa explained when Julia finally let go of him. Then he spotted Esther. *"Liebling!"* he cried, throwing his arms around her. "It is so good to see you well again."

Esther hugged him back hard. She was shocked at how his cheeks had sunk into his face. Hugging Pa reminded her of the first time she'd hugged Mickey and she'd felt every one of his bones. It frightened her how much Pa had changed.

And Ma looked so much older! Lines had taken the place of curves on her face. Her skin, like Pa's, was pasty white. She had dark shadows under her eyes.

Esther wanted to throw her arms around Ma, but she held herself back. She remembered how Ma had pulled away the last time she'd done that. So she just looked at Ma and smiled.

The creases in Ma's face lifted into a smile, too. She took a step forward. Her hands reached out and Esther's breath caught in her throat. Was Ma going to hug her at last? Esther's heart pumped faster. She took a step toward Ma.

Suddenly Walter broke away from Julia. He pushed past Violet, right between Esther and Ma. Ma's hands fell and so did Esther's heart.

Walter tugged on Esther's arm. "Guess what? I did your chores while you were gone. I collected the eggs an' everything."

Part of Esther wanted to shake her little brother. But

he was beaming up at her so proudly. He didn't know what he'd done. And his cheeks were so thin and white. She managed to smile back at him. "That's wonderful, Walter. That was very grown up of you."

Violet slipped her arm through Esther's and pulled her toward the kitchen. "Isn't this place nice?" she bubbled. "I can't believe we're finally back to civilization!"

Violet's arm was so thin, it made Esther wince to look at it. She felt a rush of shame. She had been pampered on custards and fruit. But Violet had gone hungry. Esther had opened her mouth to defend the farm. Instead she grinned and pointed. "There's the bathroom, Vi."

Violet let out a shriek. "At last!" She dashed inside and banged the door closed behind her.

Esther went back to the parlor. Kate had arrived with Henry Christian asleep on her shoulder. She was shaking her head. "Oh, Ma and Pa!" she said sadly. "You both look positively ill. I'm so glad you came home from that dreadful place."

Esther was close enough to see Pa's face clearly. His mouth smiled at Kate. But his eyes were sad beyond words.

16 Esther's Wish

WITH SO MANY HELPING HANDS, IT didn't take long for the moving truck to be unloaded and for the furniture to be set in place. The dishes, pots, and pans were washed and put away. The beds were made, and clothing was hung in closets. Walter would sleep on a cot in the girls' room until they could afford a bigger place, but no one complained about having to share.

The sun was setting behind them as they all walked back to Kate and Howard's apartment for dinner.

Walter kept running ahead and then running back to them. Once he started to run into the street. Ma had to call out, "Walter, stop!" And when she caught up to him, she scolded, "You are not in Johannsen's Corners.

There are lots of cars and trucks here. You cannot just run into the street."

"Yes, Ma," Walter said, staring wide-eyed at a streetcar that rumbled past.

Violet kept looking around as she walked beside Esther. "I can't believe we're really here!" she said. "I thought today would never come."

Esther reached out and squeezed Violet's hand. "I missed you so much!"

For a surprise, Kate was roasting a turkey. "We never did have Thanksgiving together," she said, "so I decided we'd celebrate now. After all, we have a lot to be thankful for."

Pa nodded. "Yes, we do. We are all well." He smiled at Esther. "And we are all together again—an even bigger family than we were before." He looked down at the baby on his knee. His big hand rested gently on Henry's curly head. "We are blessed."

Esther swallowed hard. She'd been feeling anything but blessed lately. But now, listening to Pa and having all her family around her again, she knew it was so. She missed the farm and the life they'd had there. But the farm was just a place. Home was more than a place. Home was family.

Later, when Kate and Julia were bringing steaming dishes to the table, Kate asked Esther to close the parlor curtains. Esther stood at the middle of the double window and grasped the edge of a curtain in each hand. But she paused before she pulled them together.

The moon was just coming up above the rooftops of the city, and it had a strangely pink glow. She opened her mouth to ask Ma what the pink glow meant. But then she closed her mouth without saying a word. Whether Ma would say the glow was a sign of something good or something bad didn't matter to Esther.

Signs might be important, even comforting, to Ma. But Esther would much rather take life one day at a time and be surprised as each day unfolded, the good and the bad by turns. With a last look at the pink moon, she closed the curtains.

She sat down and looked at each smiling face around the table, starting with Pa and ending with Ma. Had Ma been about to hug her earlier? Esther believed she was. Just as she was sure Ma had said "I love you" that night in the hospital. She might have dreamed it. But she didn't think so.

The memory warmed a special place in her heart, but it wasn't the be-all and end-all she'd thought it would be. Because she knew now that words were the smallest part of loving.

"Actions speak louder than words," her Chicago teacher, Miss Monksburg, used to say. Now those words came shining out of Esther's memory. Like sunshine, they reached down to her tangled thoughts and helped the last of them give one last mighty thrust to break through into the light. Suddenly Esther saw it all so clearly!

Love was actions more than words. And not just easy actions like hugs and kisses. It was hard ones, like sticking by someone in bad times, not just in good. It was working for them, even when you were tired. It was putting their needs first, even before your own. It was taking care of them when they were sick. It was forgiving them when they disappointed you. It was protecting them and teaching them. It was all the things Ma had always done for Esther.

"I'm so stuffed, I can't eat another bite," Walter said, sliding down in his chair.

"That will leave more cake for the rest of us," Julia teased. Everyone laughed as Walter quickly popped back up.

Julia collected dirty plates and brought out smaller ones for dessert. Then Kate came out of the pantry with the cake. Esther was surprised to see it was aglow with burning candles. Everyone began to sing: *"Happy birthday to you . . . Happy birthday to you . . . Happy birthday, dear Esther . . . Happy birthday to you!"*

Esther looked at the pink-frosted cake Kate set before her and stammered, "B-but it's not—"

"We know your birthday's not until Friday really," Kate interrupted. "But we thought you wouldn't mind celebrating early." She set a pink-and-white-wrapped package on the table. And Julia put a flat blue package beside it. A book! Esther guessed happily. Maybe even another Nancy Drew mystery.

She was all set to reach for it when Pa reminded her, "The candles, *Liebling*. Make a wish before they go out."

Esther stared at the tiny candle flames. A wish. Last year she wouldn't have had to think about it. But this year was different. She felt as if she suddenly saw things a lot more clearly even if she did still need glasses. She closed her eyes. She thought a moment and made her wish. Then she opened her eyes, took a deep breath, and blew with all her might. The candles flickered and went out. Everyone clapped. Howard whistled loudly through his teeth. Esther grinned.

"Now, open your presents," Julia said, plucking candles from the cake so she could cut it.

"This one," Ma said. She pulled a knobby bundle from beneath the table and held it out to Esther. "Open this one first."

Esther looked at Ma in surprise. She took the package, slid off the string, and began to peel away the brown paper. Her heart started to beat faster. She threw a quick glance at Ma. Was it possible? Ma's eyes urged her to continue. Esther's heart lurched. She smelled the scent of lilacs—Ma's powder. She saw a tiny hand, then a fat braid—molasses brown now, not golden anymore—and finally, two china-blue eyes.

"Margaret!" she breathed. She touched the doll's pretty dress. It was made of the same red-and-white rose-print fabric that had hung at the kitchen windows of the farmhouse. Now it would be easy to close her eyes and pretend herself back there again.

But it was Margaret's face that she stared at in wonder. It had been so horribly stained. Ma must have scrubbed and scrubbed and scrubbed. As closely as Esther looked, she could find only one small spot on Margaret's cheek. "She reminds me of Bethany." She gulped. "Thank you, Ma."

Ma nodded and smiled so wide, Esther felt as if she'd been hugged tight.

"Oh—I almost forgot!" Violet said. "I have a letter for you from Bethany." She jumped up from the table to find her coat. In a moment she was back with a crumpled envelope. Esther eagerly tore it open.

Dear Esther,

I wish I could have seen you one more time to say good-bye. You are the best friend I ever had. I miss you something awful. I wanted to be the one to tell you not to worry about Mickey. Your pa brought him over and everybody here loves him already, especially me. If you write to me, I promise to write back. And maybe sometime we can visit one another. I hope so.

Your good friend,
Bethany

Esther thought she might burst with happiness. She didn't have to worry about Mickey after all. "Thank you, Pa," she said. "Bethany will take good care of Mickey, I know."

Pa nodded.

"Now I can write letters to Bethany like I used to write to Julia," Esther added. "And she can tell me about Mickey and the kids at school."

"Aren't you going to open the rest of your presents?" Walter demanded. "I want cake."

Esther grinned. With Margaret in her lap, she opened a jigsaw puzzle from Kate and Howard. Then, just as she'd hoped, she unwrapped a Nancy Drew book from Julia. "Thank you, everybody," Esther said. "This has been a wonderful birthday party."

They all clapped their hands, even little Henry.

I will remember this birthday forever, Esther promised herself. Then she looked across the table at Ma and smiled, because at last she saw the love that had always been in her mother's eyes.

Esther picked up her fork and took a bite of cake. "This is lots better than the cake Violet made for me last year," she teased.

Violet made a face but laughed along with everyone else.

The laughter was such a nice sound. It made Esther think of the wish she'd made minutes before. Not that she believed in birthday wishes anymore, or lucky ribbons for that matter, or signs or superstitions.

Good and bad things happened all the time. Sometimes good things even came out of bad ones, like when Esther had choked but Bethany saved her and Ma let her be Esther's friend again. Or like when Ma threw Margaret away but today she gave Margaret back to Esther, a beautiful memory of their time on the farm and a very special sign of her love for Esther.

There was no harm in wishing, though, and this year Esther's birthday wish had come straight from her heart with no planning at all. She had looked at all the loving faces around the table and known that all she really wanted was for her family to stay together forever.

It was a good wish, she decided, popping another forkful of cake into her mouth. Best of all, she had a feeling it was one wish that was going to come true.

ACKNOWLEDGMENTS

With special thanks to the members of my critique group: Kathleen Ernst, Amy Laundrie, Eileen Daily, Julia Pferdehirt, Laurie Rosengren, Cindy Schumerth, Nancy Sweetland, and Lisl Detlefsen for their valuable insights and encouragement during the writing of this book—and for their treasured friendship always.

My deep appreciation to Jan Dundon, fellow children's book lover, longtime friend, and enthusiastic supporter, for all her help and for never losing faith.

And to Susan Kochan, editor extraordinaire, my eternal gratitude for believing in Esther and for enabling me to share her story with children everywhere.

GAYLE ROSENGREN grew up in Chicago. Like Esther, she enjoyed school, was a voracious reader, and loved dogs and horses. She attended Knox College in Galesburg, Illinois, where she majored in creative writing and was the editor of the literary magazine. Gayle never outgrew her passion for children's books, and she worked as a children's and young adult librarian at Fountaindale Public Library in Bolingbrook, Illinois, for several years.

Also like Esther, Gayle eventually moved to Wisconsin, but by then she was a mother with three children. She worked in a reference library and as a copyeditor, and she wrote short stories for children that appeared in *Cricket, Ladybug, Jack and Jill* and *Children's Digest* magazines. Now Gayle writes full-time just outside of Madison, Wisconsin, where she lives with her husband, Don, and their slightly neurotic rescue dog, Fiona. She is living her dream, she says, writing books she hopes will make the same difference in children's lives as her favorite authors made in hers. *What the Moon Said* is her first novel.

www.gaylerosengren.com